I0738289

Maximum Mayhem
by LM Pampuro

Maximum Mayhem
Copyright 2013 by LM Pampuro
Revised Version 2018

Maximum Mayhem is a work of fiction. Names, characters, places, or incidents either are a product of the author's imagination or are used fictitiously. Any resemblance to actual persons, living or dead, business establishments, events, or locale is entirely coincidental.

There is nothing centered in reality in this book.

ISBN: 4505787

Printed in The United States Of America

For the people who make small-town living sane:
Renee, Laura, Pat, Barry,
& of course, my Steve

Chapter One

What a day! The sun glowed, and the wind blew south away from the cow pasture, so the smell cow poop lingered in the opposite direction. What's more, I am in a mellow state of mind without the help of a good wine buzz. Karma blessed me as did my horoscope. I received this one-liner: This will be a fabulous day. What else could I possibly need?

I announced Maxi's day off yesterday after another horrendous session with my soon to be ex and his lawyer. I looked down at the band-aid on my middle finger. Before the meeting, I slammed it in the car door. I ruined the manicure I just charged forty-five dollars on my credit card, because I had to give the impression I still had it together, so I can keep my kid, boat and other things I worked my ass off for. When I rambled to my assistant, Nancy, about my ordeal, she dropped a bombshell.

"Maxi, you just got a call from Bob Carlson. Something about scheduling a lunch date for tomorrow. Should I try to postpone?"

Great! Bob Carlson is my former boss. I wondered what he wanted. "Nancy, please try to reschedule with Bob. I really need tomorrow off." Curiosity will kill me. I could deal with that later. I need and deserve to run away from work and life in general.

Nancy mumbled something as I disconnected. I had to love her. I vow here and now after this mess is over, I will send her to a spa for the day during work. I will tell her I am sending her on a sales call, so she'll actually go.

I should probably write this all down.

I closed my eyes and felt the sun on my skin. My heartbeat slows, and my breath becomes more rhythmic. The kids are playing in the pool, the buzz of a lawnmower can be heard in the distance, and just as I reach a state of ah, my friggin' cell phone rings. So close! I reach over to check the number. Crap! So much for a peaceful day.

"Hello?" I heard Gert's voice on the other end, and my body automatically tightened up. *Here we go again.* Not even twenty-four hours had passed since I freaked out in his lawyer's office. The idiot tried to get full custody of our son! Like I'd ever give that up!

Gert and I left the office and went through Jon's wish list while floating on my boat, now referred to as the U.S.S. Last Straw, in Long Island Sound. I thought the best way for a clear mind to make life-changing decisions is while breathing in the salt air. Of course, for some unknown unrealistic reason, I thought I had a reprisal. Sometimes I live in denial.

I guess Gert's call signals the beginning of the next round. I lost count of what series we were in. Why everything with him totally screwed up any attempt at the state of ordinary, I'll never understand.

"Hey, Gert, what's going on?" I pictured Gert leaning forward on her desk, with her blonde curly hair falling around her face, resting her bosom on edge. I think about Gert, the person. She is definitely a woman to reckon with. The woman is super bright, equally beautiful, but also, fortunately for me, on my side. She had been married four times, divorced twice, annulled once, and now happily widowed. She tolerated no crap from anyone, including me, which is why she took care of all my legal stuff.

Since I tend to be too sweet, I needed more than one hard-ass backing me up. Nancy's sturdy, yet when the business expanded rapidly, she needed back up also. Gert took the lead in doing market research. She accepted no crap from anyone in those areas and still managed to get the required information. She became my inspiration to be a more robust person.

It is ironic how I could run my own company and get people to do what I need, yet in my personal life, things tended to fall through the cracks. The sad part was half the time when they did; I could care less as long as the business runs smoothly.

Without preamble, her girly voice came over the line again. "That idiot you married is lower than dog puke."

"Tell me something I don't know." Here we go again. Anytime Gert started a conversation swearing, I knew I am in trouble. Truth being my ex is lower than dog puke. I'm one of those women who became single, not by choice. My soon to be ex-husband had decided after ten years of marriage he didn't want to be married anymore, at least not to me.

There is a difference.

He had met a single mom while doing freelance computer stuff or maybe at the bar frequented. I'm not sure.

I do know she's twenty-eight, had the curves in all the right places, and a libido hornier than a goat, from what little I know about goats. That is pretty horny.

Sometimes I didn't blame him for leaving. I did not wait on him and put myself at his disposal, or, better yet, spread my legs on command. He didn't understand I was busy: busy raising a child, busy growing a business, and busy keeping a household financially afloat. I was doing too much and, at the same time, not enough. Who knows! Second-guessing decisions is my middle name.

I called the new love of his life, The Tart. Her real name is Hillsey. She had a body that could've been on the cover of some fashion magazine, or at least spread out in the centerfold. Compared to my body, which is okay in some spots while lacking in others, hers belonged in *Playboy*. If my boobs were more prominent, my stomach might look flatter, and if my legs were a little longer, my butt wouldn't stick out as much.

All my body had ever needed is a few minor adjustments. I guess Jon wanted a no ass, big boob, and perky little woman. Or he just didn't want me.

Five months ago, we went out for a romantic Valentine's Day lunch. We got buzzed on martinis while overlooking the Connecticut River. A perfect winter day, with lots of sun and very little wind. Out of nowhere, he leaned across the table, took both of my hands in his, and announced our situation wasn't working for him. Stupid me thought he was going to say something corny and romantic. We went home. He packed and left.

I was surprised, angry, bitter, nauseous, and ecstatic, all at once. To have a conversation with me was like talking to five different people because my moods shifted with the wind. Some days I wanted to thank him; other days, I wanted to kill him. I tried to keep it all in check because I didn't want my ten-year-old to suffer or to think his father's an idiot.

"Did you know Jon and his sleazy lawyer just filed an injunction to claim half your business as his own?" Gert said, and then paused.

I hate it when she pauses because it will mean bad news for me.

"And he's going for the boat. Not a share of the boat like we discussed, but the whole damn vessel. He said something about it being compensation for mental abuse."

I sat up in my deck chair and checked over my shoulder on the boys. Ric didn't need to hear this. At least my brain's working. With my legs and hips making cracking sounds from sitting too long, I got up and walked towards the opposite side of the deck, faced away from the boys. I spoke at a level where my voice wouldn't carry.

"You tell dick breath he can't have the boat, and if he wants part of my business, he'll have to prove he's ever lifted a finger to make it a success. Gert, I am not giving in on either of these."

"His lawyer thought you'd say that. The word for word actually. So, here's the deal, Max. If you refuse, he said he's going to continue to fight for full custody."

"That, that, that . . ." I couldn't think of a despicable enough name to call him. I closed my eyes and listened to the sounds of the boys laughing behind me. I inhaled air all the way down into the pit of my stomach, then released it and counted silently to ten. The boys splashed away in the pool.

"No, we should do it this way," I heard my son say.

"No, Ric, put the raft in first, and then jump," Rye answered.

I glanced back at the kids to make sure they weren't doing anything foolish, as ten-year-old boys tended to do, then I continued, "Gert, what about the list and everything we went over? Can't we do something there?"

"We can. I believe we can. Maxi, I have to be honest. My gut says this it's all about the money. I hate to tell you this, but I think Jon is using Ric as leverage."

I sighed. This sucked. This totally sucked. My boat is only a thing, not necessary, but it is my last sanctuary. I used it as an escape to get away from my life. "Between you and me, I am willing to sell the boat and the business if I can find a buyer. I could then give him half, even though he doesn't deserve any of it, just to get him out of my life. That would at least be a situation I could live with. I can't take Jon away from his son, but I don't need to let him have him full time. The bottom line is the kid is what is most important to me."

I could get another boat, start a new business, and start completely over with just Ric and me. I thought about that scenario a lot, but I didn't dare say it aloud, thinking if I did, the other shoe would drop. My voice sounds squeaky and loud. The boys were quiet. Not a good sign.

14

Exhaling deeply, "Gert, just take care of it. Tell me what you need me to do, and I'll do it. As far as I'm concern, he's getting the deal of the century just playing by Connecticut law. Of course, he's too dumb to figure that out. Either way, we need to turn off the spigot, also known as my bank account."

"Gotcha. Exactly what I thought you'd say. The paperwork is ready, and we are off. I should warn you, though, it may end up being costly for you. I just needed your permission to start."

"You've got it!"

I disconnected the call, took in another deep breath, and thought about throwing my phone in the pool. I needed to calm down and feel like a normal, rational person. Jon is an idiot to even consider I would give up anything to him, especially Ric. He needed to be reminded he left us! That kid meant more to me than any of the stuff we accumulated. *Keep dreaming, buddy*, I thought. *There was no way you are going to take away my kid.*

I lay back on the chaise and breathe deeply in through my nose and out through my mouth. I glanced around my parent's back yard and tried to remember the time when I first started calling my parent's home, "The Country Club." Their property is in the middle of cow country, and my dad had always kept the lawn perfectly manicured like a golf course, much to the envy of our neighbors.

When we were younger, he built horseshoe pits along the back property line but has since grown in and been converted to a pumpkin patch. Later, he and my mother put in a garden and a small barn they called a shed. Around the pool, my dad constructed a wooden deck with built-in benches; he managed to update himself every ten years or so. Nowadays, they kept the pool going for the grandchildren. I am grateful they kept opening it up every summer.

The faint smells of the season surrounded me. Cut grass, roses, trees, and occasional whiffs of cow poop from the farm up the street fill the air. I watched my son and his friend wrestle over the blow-up rafts scattered across the water. My parents' house had always been a kind of sanctuary. Not that I've had the perfect Norman RockWell, family — far from it. We'd all developed our own quirks that come out at the worst possible times — mostly around the holidays. There wasn't much chance of family conflict in mid-July during steamy days when my brothers were all off somewhere with their families in tow.

My parents were currently hiding away in their air-conditioned house, doing whatever it is people their age do during sweltering days. I chose to bake in the sun and tan, though I am not sure why. Mostly I just sat and let my imagination run away with me. In a negative frame of mind, it can be a bad thing, a horrible idea.

I don't live here anymore. I am just a visitor. I try hard to time my visits when my brothers were not going to be around. I loved my brothers dearly, but they had a way of making me feel inferior. I had yet to figure out how, since I presented myself to the outside world as a confident woman who worked hard to run a successful business, raise a wonderful son, and try to be herself. You know – the woman has it all! But as I attempted to find my way down a path that may or may not exist, I prayed the road cleared soon, or I will

16

need to get a weed whacker out and cut through the hedges to find a clearing.

"Mom, wake up!" Ric shouted from the pool edge as he tossed water onto my legs. It felt like bathwater, not very refreshing, yet inviting either.

"I'm awake, dude. What's up?" I answered, stretching my legs out over the end of the plastic lounge chair. Since Jon left, I kept the house in the town where Ric has lived his entire existence. His life hasn't changed much. It had not been easy, but looking at my son, it has been worth it.

We lived in a cute little beach town; however, I preferred pools to the Sound. No icky slimy things live in pool water. Nor are there crabs or fish or other live creatures that might bite toes. As a bonus, no baseball moms are gossiping about us while we sunbath a few feet away.

Earlier I had floated around in the pool on one of the blow-up rafts until the boys thought it would be funny to flip me into the water. I didn't know it was as amusing as they did. My dad laughed hysterically. My dad probably instigated the flip.

Ric and Rye climbed out of the water and stood beside me, shivering in the hot summer air. "Your towels are hanging on the railing," I pointed out as they moved to grab them.

"Rye and I are hungry. Can we bug Gram for food?" Ric inquired while he dripped.

I went through my bag to find my cell phone. If they walked through the house wet, I would never hear the end of it, and to make matters worse, I would need to get up and clean up the water puddles. "Mom, the boys are hungry," I stated. I listened to her tell me she would bring snacks out in a few minutes. "Thanks." Pressing the off button, I relayed her message. "Dudes, Gram is going to bring you snacks, so dry off, and she'll be out in a few."

Ric dropped his towel and moved towards the gate. "Bet I can beat you from here to the table," he shouted at his friend.

"Bet you can't," Rye yelled back as both boys jumped over the stairs and sprinted across the grass.

Why little boys challenge each other constantly, I will never know. One always has to be the fastest, slowest, biggest, or the "best" at something all the time. I wondered if little girls were like that too. As I watched the boys chasing each other across the lawn, I thought it is way too hot to be moving that fast.

I must admit, in some ways, I know I am fortunate. I had my kid, he had his friend, and life right is okay. My plan is to swim at the club for the afternoon and then head back to the shore. With any luck, Rye's mom would volunteer to take the boys overnight. Then I could do nothing, similar to what I had been doing all day except I could do it in peace and quiet with ice cream or a container of lo mien all to myself. I don't want Ric to see my nightly tears.

As I thought about being by myself, I needed to come up with ways to spend the evening and distract my mind. I can rent an old Mel Gibson movie or read a trashy novel, that would do the trick. Along with a bottle of white wine and Chinese food to go, it could be very nice. I need to keep proving to myself over and over again after Jon left, I could and would make my life better. As anyone could see, I had succeeded.

Ha! Who am I kidding? Whenever Ric went away to a friend's or went out with his father, all I do is stay awake and worry. And it sucked! When he visited Jon's, I'd get all freaked out because I didn't know if he's there by himself with only the T.V. for company. At least when he visited his bud's house, it had a little less stressful. I knew then he was with a responsible adult.

In any case, the wine actually helped. I know I shouldn't get drunk and pass out just because my son slept in another place. Getting bombed is always a bad idea, even if it did help me sleep through the night.

My mother's hip-checked open the back door. In her hands, a tray of Cheeto's, Pringles, soda, and other combinations of foods full of additives Ric would never get at home. I stocked zero junk food except for the occasional bag of Cape Cod potato chips for my emergency P.M.S. junk food weakness. Add a few chocolate bars to the mix, and all who enter are safe from the crazy lady.

"Come and eat!" my mom's voice boomed from the patio. I look in her direction, *eat what?* She stood there in old jeans, shorts and a t-shirt, looking great for a woman over seventy. I don't know how she did it. She soaked up the sun, had smoked as long as I'd known her, and her eating habits obviously left a lot to be desired. Yet my mom is the same size and build as me. I just don't get it. I need to exercise and watch what I eat to maintain my size. As I considered my mom, it occurred to me; *maybe I do have a few genes on my side.*

Chemical cuisine is not my style, yet I forced myself up off the lounge chair, walk down the stairs, and cross the grass to have my suspicions confirmed.

She brought out nothing edible. Meanwhile, the boys licked their orange-from-the-Cheetos fingers and chugged down glasses of soda, to see who could burp the loudest and longest.

"I have other stuff upstairs," Mom said while she watched my nose crinkle at her buffet. "Do you want a sandwich? I have some nice ham."

To my mom, all food had personality traits. She's kind of cool.

"No, thanks. I'm okay. I'll eat a salad later." I reached over to get a Pringle along with a large glass of ice water she had brought out for me.

"How's the water?" My parents had had a pool for over twenty-five years ago, yet in all that time, I can't remember my mom ever swimming in it.

"It's like bathwater. You should go in," I said.

"Yeah, right." She walked back towards the house, balancing an empty bottle of soda in one hand and bags of chips in the other, "By the way, there was a phone call for you. Someone you graduated high school with. Not sure of the name. Dad talked to him."

Mom grinned and waited by the door for my next question. "So, what did this person want?" Of course, she knew I would ask.

"Not sure, he talked to Dad. I'll send him out."

She disappeared while I wondered who tracked me down. The few friends I still had from town would call me directly at home or on my cell. It had to be someone I hadn't heard from in a while. I graduated with two hundred and eighteen other people. That would narrow it down to two hundred and ten who were still alive and could possibly be the mystery caller. I would guess two hundred nine really could care less

20

what Maxi Malloni was doing since high school. This is my Virgo-ness in action, overanalyzing everything. My hand automatically snapped up and hit the side of my head. I heard the window in the kitchen slide open.

"He can't remember," my mother yelled down. "Maybe whoever called will call back." I shrugged my shoulders as she closed the window. A mystery person? How lovely. I knew my life missed some form of excitement. I mean, I thought I had it all starting with a nasty divorce, plus a business I should concentrate on more before it took a dive from neglect. Let's not forget a boat I didn't have time to use, an ordinary family I loved dearly, although entertaining would be a better description.

Along with all that, I now have a mystery person inquiring about my whereabouts. Nothing in my world made much sense anyway. So this mysterious caller could be the missing link to send me over the edge.

Chapter Two

"Oh joy," I expressed to no one. I could hear the boys wrestling on the pool deck. The splash would come soon.

"No. No, listen to me…" and back the boys went to argue. I wondered, not for the first time, how these two turned out to be best friends. I guessed this is a guy thing. I watch a bird sail through the yard. I should be reading or catching up on work. My briefcase is within reach, yet I just waddle up the stairs, sit back, and continue to watch the world go by. What I need to do is calm down. My stomach remained in motion about Gert's call. Damn son of a bitch, cheating lying piece of horse poop on a skewer. Now breathe deep, my inner voice instructed.

Hmmm, well, that didn't make me feel better, only upped my blood pressure. I want to be less angry towards Jon, but he makes it so hard! Especially when he did so many boneheaded things. I mean, I know he loves his son, but full custody? I don't think so! Think about it—how will he and Hillsey go out every night if they had to be responsible parents? Oh wait, that's right, they're not accountable.

I took another extended, slow, deep inhalation. My yoga instructor told our class deep breathing could help a person see more clearly. He also said, "It centers your body and your mind. Deep breathing puts you in touch with your inner being."

For me, his soft, deep voice had a calming effect. When I am in class, breathing deeply, everything slows down, giving me a false sense of calm. It sometimes works when I am out, of course, but not when I am riled up. Then the process only makes me dizzy.

Rye and Ric's voices faded away while my mind drifted into a sunny daydream. I could hear the bees drone in the background, the beagles barking next door, a tractor in the distance, and the back door opening and closing. I probably should've opened my eyes to see who came out, but then again, why bother? My mom or dad was perhaps just puttering around. They would wander over eventually.

The boys had gotten awfully quiet. I peeked out to make sure they hadn't drowned each other.

"No, Ric, you breathe this way,"

"No way, Rye, it's better my way."

Okay, I shouldn't giggle, but the way they fight one never knew.

"Hey, is your mom around?" an unfamiliar voice inquired with the boys.

I could see through the glare Ric pointed towards me, the slug in the lounge chair. I followed his gaze to just below the stairs and, of course, couldn't see a face. I could see a person dressed in tan khaki pants and a white polo shirt. Not anyone I recognized. Most of my friends were probably working midweek, not stalking me at my parents' place. Clunking footsteps moved up the stairs, and the gate creaked as he came through it. I moved to see his face.

Hard features and dark eyes, similar to those of a bad boy in the movies. Speaking of film, he definitely is handsome enough to be in the movies! My hand automatically hit my forehead as the reality of a movie star visiting me sets in.

"Doesn't that hurt?" the stranger asked.

"Only when I do it right," I say with a smile.

He moved closer to sit on the bench next to me. His eyes were either watching my legs or the boys. I couldn't tell from his position, and it would be too obvious for me to cover myself up. I am relieved to be wearing a two-year-old tankini that almost hid my midsection, as opposed to the bikini I usually wear in the backyard. I might not look like Hillsey, with an Italian gene pool like mine that would be impossible without starvation or liposuction. Still, I do look younger than a forty-one-year-old woman going through a significant life crisis.

He folded over and rested his arms on his thighs. "Your brother said you were around, so I called your parents for a number. Lucky for me, you happened to be here."

I still don't know this person.

"So, I figured since your dad said to come on over, I would. I hope this isn't a bad time." He glanced down at me and beamed.

I had to admit, this guy had a great smile. The smile looked somewhat familiar. Maybe?

"Uh, no. My dad said, come on over, huh?"

Leave it to my dad, who couldn't remember the guy's name but invited him over anyway. Dad still saw me as someone who needed to be taken care of. God forbid I should end up a strong, independent woman

24

without a husband! Yeesh. My dad would think I had decided to become a lesbian, or there must be something wrong with me if I didn't want a man around. He probably considered this guy as a potential hubby number two. Little did Dad know I had vowed never, ever, ever, to get married again. Marriage, as it turned out, is a fairy tale for some, but a sham for Jon and me.

I give my head a shake before refocusing on the stranger. "So, what are you up to these days?" Maybe his answer would give me a clue. My butt stuck to the plastic lounge chair, and I knew if I got up, there would be red marks across my backside. This guy is too cute to see red marks on my butt so early in our acquaintance.

"Not much. I guess Pete told you I work for the government, too. I ran into him down in D.C. a lot during the last year."

He knew Pete. That made him closer to my age. Good clue, dude. Pete's my younger brother. Mr. Perfect as a child and unfortunately for me, still Mr. Perfect as an adult. My parents' pride and joy, one might say. Pete tried to explain to me once what he did for a living, something for Uncle Sam and the Navy, but I never understood what he is talking about. He spoke way too technical for me, probably on purpose. He had a huge title, in charge of a lot of people, and made piles of money came from my tax dollars. I'm glad my tax dollars are funding my brother's lavish lifestyle. To whom did he meet up within D.C.? I couldn't remember him mentioning meeting any old friends of mine or, for that matter, of his. Pete's memory must be like my dad's—nonexistent. Damn genetics.

"Do you live in D.C.?" I asked. We were starting to play that kids game, Guess Who. The players asked a series of questions to find out what person you had on your secret card. You eliminated options as the items are answered, and the one who guessed correct first won. I tried to remember what came next after, "Does he have blonde hair?"

I shifted my weight to face him. I also wanted to lift up to allow air between the chair and my butt. I figured the way things are moving with the conversation. Eventually, I'd need to stand. "Pete goes there quite a bit on business." I fished like a pro.

"No, I lived down south but moved back here about six months ago. You know, parents getting old and such. Now I just go down to D.C. on business once in a while."

"Really? What kind of business?" Now I am getting somewhere. I could match the occupation with the person. I glanced up at his face and sighed. Maybe not.

"I do work for the military, kind of like Pete does. I'm lucky with computers and all, I can work from anywhere and just attend meetings every so often. How about you?"

Well,, that didn't work. "Oh me? I publish a guide down at the shore for the visitors." I waved my hand as I spoke. "It makes life easier doing your own thing with kids, you know."

"They are both yours?"

"Just me." Ric shivered next to my chair. Rye already had a towel wrapped around himself and heading back to the junk food. "I'm Ric," my son said. He held out his hand to shake.

26

"I'm Zack," the stranger replied, as he shook Ric's extended hand. "I'm an old friend of your mom's."

That satisfied Ric. He smiled and took off to search for Cheetos.

"Cute kid."

"Yeah, but don't let him fool you. He's a hellion," Zack, who, I wondered. I only knew one Zack from high school. How could I ever forget that guy? I had a severe crush on him and couldn't walk by the guy without blushing or giggling. I seriously doubt he would be sitting on my parents' deck so many years later. Could I be napping, and all this is a dream. Ric is at Rye's house, and this hallucination is nothing more than the beginning of a hangover from Mondovi Chardonnay. I shift my body to look more intently at the guy sitting next to me.

Visualize, Maxi! If you made the hair a little longer, maybe slimmed the gut a bit, and took away the hardness in the face, it could be Zack. "Do you have any kids?" I still wanted more information because the guy who flashed in my mind would never be sitting on my parents' pool deck.

"Yes, I have two girls, but both are living elsewhere. One's in college in Boston, and the other is in the process of moving to L.A. with her mother. She's going to be an actress or something stupid." He leaned back against the railing. "I guess I started earlier than you."

"I guess so, but I bet I had more fun in my twenties." I sat taller in the chair, and then start to giggle, both a nervous reaction and a flashback to my wild and free twenties. I had loved my twenties. Man, did I have fun! If it wouldn't mean not having Ric, I could have lived my twenties forever or at least till I lost my stamina.

"I bet you did. The last time we spoke, you were heading out to see a band play. I wish we had hooked up then." His voice trailed off.

"Seeing a band, huh?" I giggled again. When did that annoying junior high school girl sound return? "That could be any night. So, what brings you here?" Okay, so subtleties are not my strong point. Besides, if this is THE Zack Brady from high school, then I wanted to know why after all this time, he sat next to me on my parents' deck?

His comment about the band brought it all back. Years ago, I had spent a long afternoon on the phone with this dude who wouldn't give me the time of day in high school. We had chatted away the hours. He said he would call the next day to get together. He never did. Not that I ever spent time wondering why he didn't. Please understand I did not.

I just had a memory of a pleasant conversation one afternoon while living in my condo. As a matter of fact, Zack called my parents that day to get my number, and they gave it to him. Odd, because this is unusual. They'd always take a number then leave me a message. Definitely strange. So why had he looked me up after so many years? I am at the point when I had enough male-related problems, and looking at Zack, this is definitely one more coming to call.

"Hey, so what brings you over?" I am so smooth.

"I was in town, so I thought I'd look up an old friend."

Not a very good line. He should come up with a better one since we were not exactly in the 'old friends' category.

"When we talked last, I was being shipped out to the Gulf later that week." He sat back and started to explain. "I didn't tell you why I was back? Anyway, I got back to Virginia with my unit about six months later and met Karen, my ex-wife. She had Lilly the college student already, and we got married a few months later because Gracie, the actress, was on the way."

Okay, now this is getting better. Could it all be bullshit, though? I bet he is a con artist. I mean, a twenty-something body on a forty-something guy is always suspicious. No gut, no butt. He still had his hair and his hair is gorgeous, just the right length. Man, if this guy played guitar…

"Karen decided she had had enough of all of us about ten years back and moved to Florida. The girls and I lived in Virginia until about six months ago when my mom got sick. Now I live here, and they live all over."

"Wow, what a ride."

"Yeah."

He still had great dimples when he grinned, and I could see the same look that sent younger me over the edge. Wonderful. Here we go again, I thought. Make my heart melt, buddy. Stupid horoscope!

"As I said, I was in D.C. and ran into Pete, who mentioned you were single again…"

"Not yet. I have a soon-to-be ex." I looked around Zack to see if Ric and Rye were still on the patio consuming junk food. I tried so hard not to be the typical ex who crucified the idiot she divorced, especially in front of the results of that union. I mean, come on, the kid had the idiot's genes in him too. "He's hauling my behind back into court on a few technicalities, so I am still married."

"Oh. Well,, in Pete's world, you dumped a loser," Zack said, holding up his hands to soften the insult. "Those were his words, not mine. He said you're moving on to a better life."

"That sounds like Pete." I nodded.

"I guess dinner would be out then?"

Did he just ask me to dinner? Wow! I had been waiting since my thirteenth birthday for this guy to ask me out on a date. How cool is this? I pinched my arm just to make sure I didn't fall asleep, and this is all in my imagination. I gave myself a red mark and significant pain. Nope, this is real.

"Why?" Oh yeah, here we go. Maxi, Maxi, Maxi, why can't you ever just let something be? Okay, I admit it. I just didn't want to wonder why he asked me out ten years from now. In reality, if he is as smooth as he appears, he will just make something up. I just wished guys would come out with the truth and say: I need sex, and I heard from your brother you might be desperate. Wouldn't that make things less complicated? I watch him sitting there. He has wrinkles on the top of his nose. Could that be a thinking pose? It is kind of funny and definitely cute. I couldn't remember if he had that look like a teenager. Probably not since he wouldn't have had wrinkles back then.

Zack inhaled deeply, "I just thought it would be nice to spend time with an old friend. Nothing more." He looked a little off balance like he expected me to jump at the chance to go out with him. "I understand if you're busy."

"Well,, not exactly busy…" I stared at the ground as I heard my mother's voice from the kitchen window.

"We'll take the boys," she called. I guess her hearing is better than I thought.

"Thanks, Mom." I waved over to her and added, "Shouldn't that window be shut with the central air and all?" Bam! The sound of the window being slammed down echoed over the back yard.

Zack started laughing, not that I blamed him. My family could be very comical at times. Sometimes my life is just one big loony bin. "So, what's so funny?" I question in my tough girl voice, trying to act as if everything just took place is normal for everyone, not just my family.

"You still didn't answer my question. Dinner? I'll pick you up around seven?"

I entered one of those weird moments, like a dream sequence in a movie. The pool water stood still to give the illusion one could walk across it. The air whispered warm and inviting. The birds even stopped chirping as if waiting on my answer. Wow. I figured the silence as a sign. A sign of what, I had no clue. Before I could help myself, I answered, "Okay, seven it is. Can you make it someplace casual?" Unconsciously I bit my lower lip.

"Awesome." His dimples continued to throw me for a loop.

"One question," I said, and Zack gestured for me to proceed, "Do you play guitar?"

He started chuckling before responding, "Badly."

"Until then." Zack stood to leave, reached over and lifted my hand to his lips, gently brushing it before letting go. He left my hand shaking.

Chapter Three

A rational state of mind assisted me in preparing for any business situation, however, trying to be sensible at my parents' house is impossible, especially when I am getting ready for an "Oh God," date. After Zack left, I hauled my sagging butt inside and called my brother Pete. As usual, I reached a series of answering machines: home, office, cell, work cell, and of course, his secret government-issued pager. I text messaged him to call me A.S.A.P. This time, I wanted the real scoop on this guy instead of wondering why he called me after so many years.

I got the okay from Rye's mom to leave him with my parents for the evening. She even offered to pick them up for a sleep-over. I told her thanks, but no thanks. I would bring the boys home. No way did I want a sleep-over option after the sizzle Zack's kiss sent through my hand. I never slept with anyone on a first date. I didn't want the temptation looming over me, especially when we started at my parents' house. That would be bad. That would put me in the desperate slut category, a category no respectable Catholic girl should ever find herself in.

Plus, I didn't know what he wanted, and the way my life moved, I'm suspicious of people's motives.

Fortunately, or unfortunately, I am an inquisitive person, and this is one of those times when curiosity got the best of me. Just like back in high school, Zack could ask me to do just about anything, and I would have said yes. They say history tends to repeat itself. I should feel fortunate the only history here is on the side of my imagination.

"Okay, guys, here's the deal." I watch Ric and Rye grin at each other. "Grandma and papa are making you dinner, and you're going to hang out here for a while."

"Sounds great, mom."

"I want no problems," both boys nod.

"So, be nice to your grandparents."

"No prob, ma," Ric answered. He grabbed his backpack and headed into the back bedroom to change. Rye followed close behind, opting for the bathroom.

"Do I need to shower?" he asked.

"No. You'll probably swim again later." The door opens to Rye's outstretched hand with a wet bathing suit. In the back-bedroom, Ric's is on the floor. "Going to the mall, Mom!" I yelled as I tossed both suits on the front walk to dry in the afternoon sun.

Shopping goes against all my sane genes. When I need something, I usually called my mom, and she found it on sale for me. Today I am in an extreme situation. I couldn't trust my mother to buy anything I'd be comfortable in as if such a garment could even exist under such circumstances.

I park in front of the mall. Walk past all the chain stores, until I reach the one unchain store, Blue Moon. I wander through the sandalwood scented aisles to a clothing rack against the back wall. I grab the first dress that catches my eye and head back towards the cashier.

I use my business credit card to buy a long, beautiful, free-flowing cotton hippie dress to hide my body flaws. However, at this point, that didn't matter. Zack had already seen my body up close at the pool. The colors combined purples, blues, greens, and black. Dark colors make a person look skinnier, or so I've been told.

I get back to my parent's, jump in the shower, and do the hair thing, which in my case consists of combing it out and letting it dry. I call this the natural look. I chose not to bother with the beauty parlor stuff. I took advantage of my mom's good hair genes.

I hear my mother coming down the stairs.

"Maxi," her voice carries.

"In here." My mom walked in, and I wait for her reaction.

"Is that what you're wearing?" I got the teenage-girl-stare-down from my seventy-plus mother.

"Uh, yeah."

"Did you want to borrow a pair of sandals or a touch of makeup?" Which is my mother's polite way of saying I hate your shoes, and you need to dress your age.

"Nope, I think I'm all set." I bit down on my lip and looked in the mirror as any self-confidence I had followed my mom out the door. As if I wasn't nervous enough already.

At five of seven, I thank heaven my parents live in a huge house, which made it easy for me to hide. I am in one of the lower level bedrooms, referred to as a guest room. They converted most of the former bedrooms into other uses. The house now has an office, a sitting room and, my favorite since it took over my old room, a junk room. This is where they put all the stuff they didn't know what to do with, yet they can't throw away. Old small appliances, lawn furniture, clothes, dishes, file cabinets, and more collect dust out of sight, just in case they need it someday.

I had actual butterflies in my stomach, and as each minute ticked by, I chewed on a different nail. I should have said no. I had enough problems without inviting a new man into my life. I gave myself a reflexive head slap. But then I would wonder, wouldn't I? After all, I still wondered about the phone call to my condo years ago. I supposed I could ask him about that. Oh yeah, how pathetic could I be? Gee, Zack, since you remember a phone call way back when can you tell me why you made it? After all, I deserve to know since I've been thinking about it all this time. That would sound so lame!

Maybe I am going off the deep end. That could be justified since my life is such a mess. I need to start seeing a shrink. Talking to someone besides Gert about all my problems might be helpful. Then again, why doubt Gert just because Nancy does? Nancy had been right about a lot of stuff, but this is Gert we're talking about…Horse manure, the doorbell rang.

At least he didn't stand me up. Now there's a positive thought.

"Maxi!" Mom's voice rang through the house. If my mother is looking for me, that meant Zack and my father are conversing. Trying to limit embarrassment is a strong motivator for me to not run away. Although I could easily go out of the back door and sneak around to my car in the driveway. Like I've never done that before. I could drive away from the entire ordeal. Tempting, but my feet carried me up the stairs.

The scene I walk in on is priceless. Zack sat on the couch next to my father's chair while Ric, what a great kid I have, is grilling him. My dad must have given him pointers because he is on a roll.

"So, where are you taking my mom?" He rocked on the heels of his feet.

"I thought we'd go out to eat and then maybe catch a band somewhere if that's okay with you?" Zack and Ric both glanced at my dad, who nodded his head affirmatively.

"What time should I expect her home?" Ric sounded so grown up. When did that happen?

"What time would you like her home, sir?" Oh, this is too much.

"Well, let's say ten o'clock because we are driving south tonight."

My dad interrupted his snicker. "Ric, you and Rye are staying here, and I know your mom knows her way home in the dark."

You go, Dad. He directed the last line at Zack. "I think you could give them a later curfew. Maybe leave it up to your mom. She is, after all, over eighteen."

Dad went into full-blown laughter, which made Ric crack up too.

"Okay," Ric said. His voice became serious again. "I want my mom back, so you better take good care of her."

Zack glanced at my father, who gave Zack the glare he bestowed upon every guy who ever picked me up for a date. I should step in to stop this, but like my mom in his early seventies, my dad still intimidated. Besides, this is too funny to stop. I managed to enter casually without tripping over the door jam.

"Hey, I'm ready." I swore I heard Zack say, 'Thank God' under his breath. I walked over to Ric and gave him a big squeeze while he struggled to get. "Be good for Gram and Pop," I land a sloppy kiss on his cheek. "You too, Rye." Rye waved from across the room, where he concentrated on something on the television.

"Mom, stop it!" Ric screamed, still snorting.

"Thanks again," I said to Mom and Dad, giving my father the 'I can't believe you just did that' look. The sparkle in his eyes told me he enjoyed every minute. I guided us out the door into the humid summer air.

"That was fun," He laughed while running his fingers through his hair. "I think your dad has trained your son in the art of intimidation."

"That was nothing. My dad has cleaned his gun in front of one of my dates, did an old-fashioned interrogation on intentions to another, completely ignored a few, and, of course, did the 'Archie Bunker' I am in charge routine from his chair. If you had dated me in high school, you would have known to be prepared."

"Yeah, well, we all made mistakes in high school," Zack acknowledged wryly.

Chapter Four

"How did you ever find this place?" I followed Zack and the hostess through a maze of hanging vines, past a bamboo bar, over to a wicker table and chair set in the corner. Soft jazz music played in the background, and the arrangement of the plants gave each table its own private sanctuary. "This is so cool!" I commented. "I feel like I'm in Key West again."

"Rich suggested it."

"Rich?" My mind went blank.

"Yeah, Rich Taylor, from high school. Do you remember him?"

"Vaguely. I try to forget those years." I pick up the menu and pretended to study the items, hoping for a change in the subject. I hated high school. I never fit into any group. I had a massive crush on the guy sitting next to me, and, to be honest, I was kind of a bitch. In high school, it is essential to have a boyfriend, and you know what they say: If you can't be with the one you love, love....

It could have been worse. Zack never dated anyone steady, so at least I didn't have to put up with that kind of envy. "Do you keep in touch with a lot of folks from back then?"

"Not really. I just bumped into Rich at the grocery store. You know the line, 'Let's get together,' then it never happens."

"Sometimes, it's better." I flashed back to the damn phone call again.

"Sometimes, it's not."

He stared into my eyes, and I wondered if he could read my mind. Hum could be interesting. At least I wasn't thinking about sex. Zack's mouth turned up into a sly smile. What a great smile! I'd say yes to just about anything if he asked with that smile. What am I doing? I blush like he knew I am thinking about sex.

My hand automatically slapped the side of my head. Zack cracked up.

"My gosh, Maxi, I wonder what runs through your head when you do that."

"Just random thoughts." I grinned. No teeth, all lips. Totally fake. The look made me appear completely insane.

I brought my attention back to the menu. Pan-seared crab cakes, mahi-mahi with apricot chutney, vegetarian stroganoff, chicken picotta served over garlic mashed potatoes, fresh spring rolls, salmon grilled with maple syrup. Oh My! Choosing would be difficult.

"Zack, this menu is awesome! What are you having?"

"I'm not sure. I was advised to ask about the specials." My cell phone buzzed. I dug it out of my purse to look at the number. Crap.

"Excuse me, please. I need to answer this." With a deep breath and a painted smile, I got up from the table and headed towards the lady's room. I walked into the tiled enclave and pressed answer. "Hello, Gert.

Shouldn't you be home now?" The clock read almost eight.

"Yes, I should, but I am working for you. The former love of your life wants a meeting Tuesday at eleven. Can you make it?" I leaned against the blue and white tiled countertop to watched myself in the mirror. Could that haggard person be me looking back?

"And what pray tell does the former love of my life want?" With the mention of my ex, I immediately fall into a hostile party alert. Here I am on a nice date with a gorgeous looking guy. I knew something would go wrong.

"I believe Jon Jacobs wants to make a deal. According to Luke—that's his lawyer's real name, by the way—Jon has decided this has gone on long enough, and he is concerned about Ric. He said the situation has been too hard on the kid, and he wants to make an offer."

"What does he want, Gert? This has to be a ploy." Feeling something cool, I looked down at my dress and noticed a wet mark right around my stomach line from where I leaned. Great, just great.

"I agree. I tried to, but his pond sucking sleaze bag lawyer isn't talking. Do we want a meeting?"

Without hesitation, I answered, "Yeah, we want the meeting, either at your office or a neutral place. I don't want to go back to Luke's office. The place gives me the creeps." I moved away from the sink, so a young woman in a waitress's uniform could lean in and wash her hands. "I'm warning you, Gert, if he continues to come after Ric or my business, I will castrate him in court. This is the last straw." The woman gave me a friendly smile while fixing her make up.

"Got it. So, what are you doing? Wine and a romance novel?" Isn't the ability to transfer yourself into a different situation while remaining where you are a talent? Maybe that is only true when you're not on a date. I remembered I had left Zack sitting at the table when I answered the phone. My hand met the side of my head again.

"No, actually, I am out with an old friend. I'd better go. Talk to you later." I could hear Gert asking questions as I end the call. I looked back in the mirror once again and sighed. When did I get those wrinkles around my eyes? As I made my way towards the door, the woman in a waitress uniform stopped me.

"I didn't mean to eavesdrop on your conversation, and I know my advice is unsolicited, I need to tell you, don't give in. I did and lost part of my alimony just to get the whole thing over. Now I work two jobs while my ex goes out every night partying and forgets he has kids. Be tough."

I hugged the woman. No one should be in her situation. "Write down this number," I recited Gert's office phone. "This is my lawyer's number, and if there is a way to go back to court, she will bleed your ex dry. This kind of stuff gets her going."

The woman smiled as she headed toward the bar. I took in a deep, cleansing breath as I strolled under the vines back to the table. Zack is on his phone as I approached. I heard him say, "Got to run," as he ended the call.

"Sorry about that. Lawyer crap." I said as I slid onto the seat next to him, and absentmindedly brushing my arm against his. All my arm hairs stood up with the electricity.

Zack nodded. "Anything I can do?" He leaned closer to me, resting his chin in his left hand.

"Know a decent hitman?" I tried to laugh, but it came out fake. I helped myself to a slice of bread, noticing his brow crinkled. Is this a look of concern or confusion on his face? "Just kidding. It's been tough, and I just want the whole thing over, you know?"

"Been there, sort of, but we didn't fight. We just split everything up. I went to court one day, and an hour later, my marriage was just over." He stuffed more bread into his mouth. "Even negotiating Gracie's visitation rights came easy."

"Lucky you." The waitress returned to read the specials: coconut shrimp with apple chutney, crab California rolls, beet soup with carrots, sea bass in orange cream sauce with wild rice, Angus beef in mushroom garlic sauce with horseradish mashed potatoes, chicken rolled up with spinach and ricotta filling. I looked over at Zack.

"Okay," he answered. The waitress looked confused and, to tell you the truth, so am I. "If it's okay with you, Max, we would like one of each, substituting crab cakes for the shrimp."

"Sounds great." I am going to be in food heaven. The waitress left, and for the first time, awkward silence took over. I sipped my iced tea, fidgeted in my chair, and closed my eyes, thinking this all must be a dream. Perfect place, perfect food, perfect man, and perfect man? Where the heck did that come from? "Zack, what made you stop by today?" Okay, so I'm not smooth, and I figured the curiosity would bother me more than his answer.

"After talking to Pete, I just figured . . ."

"What?"

"Just figured I'd take a chance and see if you'd like to hang out. Why?"

"Just wondering." I twirled my straw in my drink. I wanted more information but realized I am not going to get it. I watch him look around the room, and then he focusses his gaze back on me.

"Maxi, do you remember speaking on the phone a few years after we graduated high school?" His hand casually reaches over to take hold of mine. He strokes his thumb over the top of my knuckles, lightly caressing.

"That was a long time ago, Zack. I can't remember what I had for dinner last night, never mind what I was doing then." I laughed. I remembered the call. Let's see, just about twenty years ago, midafternoon, and I lived in my little condo. I was napping to get ready to go out that evening when the phone rang. We talked for two hours about life and our lives. I invited him to meet me at the bar my musician friends were playing that night. Still, he had no ride and picking him up didn't feel right, at least my gut said at the time, so I suggested he call me at my parents on Sunday and we could meet for coffee. He agreed he would, and of course, he never called. I'd been curious why he never bothered calling since then. Not that I thought about it much, but, hey, this could be one mystery solved.

"Well,, I called you, and we talked for, gosh, a long time. It was great to catch up. You were busy, and I was shipping out a week later so… I figured you had your life, and I had mine, which got complicated after I got back. Anyway, after seeing Pete, I started to wonder what you were up to again, so I called."

"Oh." Not brilliant, but I didn't know what else to say.

"Haven't you ever wondered about something from your past?" He held both my hands. I tried to keep my body from shaking.

Only you, I thought. "Not really. I'm a fate and destiny kind of girl." The waitress returned with the crab cakes, California rolls, and soup, saying the rest would be out soon. I popped a mini crab cake in my mouth and savored the rich buttery flavor. Next came a piece of California roll. I noticed the portions were considered gourmet, which to me, is just an excuse to make them small. I was grateful Zack ordered so much.

"This is terrific," I try to keep the conversation going while reaching with my spoon to try the soup. Even being a big beet fan, I am surprised to find it tastes more like a carrot than borscht.

"Excellent choice. I'll need to thank Rich if I see him again." Zack finished off the crab cakes. He spooned the soup into his mouth as he spoke. Just the fact he would eat beet soup impressed me. When I first met Jon, the hippie, his dining cuisine leaned toward health food vegetarian earthy-crunchy type stuff. Tofu, macrobiotic seaweed, lots of beans, and vegetables without sweets or meat. After we got married, he changed to what he called "normal food." What he considered an excellent dinner had some sort of dead animal, potato, and corn with disgusting globs of butter. Nothing added or subtracted. He wouldn't eat anything exotic, even if he had never tried it—just another one of those little things that irritated me.

"Please do. I avoid the supermarket when I'm in town. I probably won't be bumping into Rich." I look down into an empty soup bowl. Bummer. I glanced up, expecting to see a ceiling, yet instead, I saw a moonlit sky. I had forgotten we were out on the deck. "Great night. Check out all those stars," I am usually not nervous around people, whether I knew them or not. I mean, come on, I'm in sales. I go to events where I didn't see a soul, walk over, and just start conversations. But my stomach had been doing somersaults ever since Zack picked me up. At least it's not nausea. My body just tingled all over.

"Yeah, it is a great night." I peeked over to Zack. He's watching me. We were heading into the awkward moment situation again. Still, before I could suggest a conversation topic, he leaned over the table and placed his mouth on mine. He tasted like beets and crabmeat, and wow, he sent my head spinning round and round. I forgot where we were and wrapped my arms around his neck. My brain went light and dizzy. There were blue flashes all around. Sparkling blue dots and stars. I behaved like a thirteen-year-old who had never been kissed. How did I ever get so lucky? I couldn't believe it. Me, Mary Alexis Malloni-Jacobs, finally in the arms of Zack Brady, after so many years. Wow.

The kiss deepened, as Zack flitted around my mouth with his tongue. His ex must have been a great kisser because he sure is no slouch in the makeout department.

How did I get so lucky? Wait a minute, how did I get so lucky? My senses went on high alert, and I jumped back at the same time Zack broke our kiss. He peered into my eyes. My hand hit the side of my head. What am I thinking?

"I don't usually get that reaction from my kisses," he said in a low voice. The heat turned on high, and my bright red face. I tried to smile yet instead started to think about how I just blew the moment.

"You're an excellent kisser." I bent over the table, grinning.

"So that makes you want to hit yourself? Maxi, I would love to know what goes on in that head of yours." Did he say, love? "I mean you and I hung out for what, three hours tops in the last twenty years, and I watched you whack yourself, how many times?"

I decided to ignore the conversation and just stare at him with a goofy smile on my face, to fool him. Maybe he'd shut up and kiss me again. Wait, did I want him to kiss me again? "I guess my new job is to find out."

I giggled at the thought. There's a possibility. Maybe he would discover something weird about me. Unconsciously I rolled my eyes toward the sky. This whole night is so strange. I had to be hallucinating and would soon wake up alone in my bed with a headache to beat the band and a half-empty bottle of wine sitting on the nightstand. It would be like every other night since Jon left. I would dream about some long-lost love I should have kept. Maxi's list of losers I had been calling them. But wait, Zack Brady was never on my list of losers. I wondered why. Maybe because he never actually dated me?

I stretched my arms over my head and found myself back in his. "Tell me about your ex."

"Why spoil the mood?" I draped my arms around his shoulders. I don't think I had never shown so much affection towards another human in public. Since I tended to be a little on the uptight side, this is very un-Maxi like and very strange, yet not uncomfortable.

"Just making conversation, I told you about mine." He grinned, showing those great dimples again.

"Strange subject, but I'll go with it. We met about twelve years ago at a concert."

"Who was playing?" His arm rested on my shoulder while his hand played with my hair. It got difficult to concentrate on the details of my life.

"Guess?" I saw the confusion on his face. Right, he didn't know anything about me since we graduated high school. "The Grateful Dead. I was in Landover, Maryland, at the time. Interesting place, Landover. It's like the ultimate suburb because the whole town was totally planned out before it was built. Very bizarre place, very structured. Anyway, he seemed like a nice guy, so we hooked up, so to speak. We would see each other on weekends mostly. He would travel up from Virginia to see me. I'd go down there. It was what it was."

"But you married him." More food arrived. The waitress arranged everything on the opposite side of the table. The smell of garlic mixed with the other spices intoxicates the air. I lunged over with my fork and scooped up a mouthful of horseradish-mashed potatoes.

"Heavenly," I sigh. After we both took entrée samples, I went back to my story. He might as well hear the truth. I figured I had nothing to lose at this point. "I married him because I was pregnant with Ric. I was too scared to be a single mom, and the alternatives didn't feel right to me. Jon wasn't a bad person. He was just carefree. I guess that would be the right description." The orange sauce from the sea bass had just the right amount of tang to it. "This is really great." Zack gestured with his fork for me to continue. "We got married, and he moved up here. I had a better job. He was into hanging with the baby. It worked. Then after Ric went to preschool, he decided to go back to school. Now he pretends to do computer stuff. He wanted to set up a business network for me, but I'm a little paranoid about modern technology. I passed. I'm not sure what he's doing now. I only know he met…" I stopped talking and concentrated on eating. I couldn't tell Zack he is sitting with such a loser. Her husband left her for a twenty-eight-year-old waitress whose bra size is more significant than her I.Q.

"He works with computers, huh?" Zack lifted his fork to offer me a spoonful of the chicken and ricotta. I closed my eyes to savor the after spice of basil and garlic floating through my senses.

Finally, I opened my eyes again. "Yeah," I answered, acknowledging what I knew of Jon's current occupation.

"Tell me about your business," Zack encouraged, changing the subject again.

My smile is real. "About five years ago, I got tired of working for someone else, so I decided to quit. I went back to school, got a Masters in writing, and after trying a lot of different things, I went back to what I knew, publishing. I started *The Guide* about three years ago and expanded it into at least one new market twice a year. It's fun."

I observed Zack chewing his food slowly. I wondered what he's thinking about. "What is *The Guide?*"

I chuckled. Why would he know what I publish? "I started with a menu guide to the shoreline. Since we were popular with the tourists, some of the attractions and stores started to advertise. My guides are in Boston, Newport, and the Connecticut coast. In two years, the goal is to be in ski country, New Hampshire and Vermont. I take care of Connecticut myself. The others are sold and written by commissioned reps. I started off doing the shoreline solo, but because of our growth, I actually had to hire a few folks."

"Wow, Maxi. That sounds like a lot of work."

"Yes and no. I work hard during the selling cycles, which are the opposite of the actual tourist season. Once we are in season, I leave it up to my assistant Nancy to take care of the day to day things. This way, I can coach baseball, hang out at the beach, and do important things with Ric. That's what it's about. The business just pays the bills."

"You have the right attitude." The plates of food had disappeared, and although my stomach is full, I didn't remember eating anything after the sea bass. "Dessert?" Zack inquired.

"I couldn't eat another bite." Sugar made me loopy. To get drunk in front of someone you hardly know is embarrassing enough, but getting a sugar buzz and having to explain why, without drinking any alcohol, well, that would be just too much, even for me. Zack signaled for the check, and all too soon afterward, we stood at my parents' door. I wanted another hot kiss, like at the restaurant, but Zach leaned over and gently touched his lips to my cheek.

"Thanks for a great evening," I said. I actually had fun, which is quite a rarity these days.

"You're welcome," he answered while still holding on to my hand. We stood for a few minutes in silence. I could hear *Sponge Bob Squarepants* on T.V. in the living room, along with boy laughter in stereo. "Can I call you again?" he asked as his lips hit mine.

I reached into my purse and pulled out a business card. "The office number rings in my house too," I instructed. Now he has my office, cell phone, office house phone, fax, and email address. No excuses not to call again this time, buddy, I thought.

"This time I won't wait another twenty years."

Chapter Five

Here it is Monday, and instead of catching up on the piles from Maxi's Day Off, I sit in a pretentious restaurant with my ex-publisher and former boss.

This is a mystery meeting.

What appeared to be a casual get together is actually a business lunch. So far, we had engaged in nothing but small talk. "How's Ric? What are your kids doing? You look great." As complimentary as Bob is, our conversation topics were much too light. I wondered what he really wanted.

I am suspicious for a good reason. I knew from working for Bob that he never did anything without a motive, especially taking people out for casual lunches during the workweek. Lesson one: When you work for Bob Carlson, everybody wants something.

When Nancy called to reschedule our original date, he went right for today. His schedule is never this clear. I moved stuff around to be here because curiosity started to get the best of me. I loved the invitation he left. "Maxi, Bob Carlson here. I just wanted to call and congratulate you on your little publication and take you to lunch to celebrate it." He's up to something.

My "little publication" had been out for more than two years. I'd say he had just happened to notice

52

that my little publication had taken some of his ad dollars. He could be pretentious, but I liked the guy. I didn't know many people who could look so casual in a custom-made Armani suit. If nothing else, Bob had always been a straight shooter, and I expected nothing less today.

"So, Maxi, give a callback, will you? I look forward to seeing you at the club."

Yep, that's Bob, alright. He wants to celebrate my success along with a free lunch at the most obtrusive restaurant he could find. We will play whatever game we were playing on his turf.

I glanced around the room and noticed the little things that made this location pretentious. For instance, the restaurant is located on a golf course in an affluent suburb of Hartford. The wait staff is trained to kiss your butt even if you were rude or obnoxious. I could imagine the back room where they'd gather and make fun of the customers' mispronunciation of the *haute cuisine* on the menu.

In what other types of dining establishment did one find such an abundance of silverware arranged across white linen tablecloths? I counted three forks, two knives, two spoons, a water glass, a wine glass, a cordial glass, and, of course, the all-important bread plate. This is a members-only place, no outsiders allowed. There are no lunch specials, just a daily customized and limited menu of fancy food that no real person eats for dinner, let alone lunch. Really, who eats pan-seared tuna with shallots and white wine served over broccoli rabe? Or better yet, Cornish game hens with sausage cornbread stuffing and fruit compote served with basil mashed potatoes. I like gourmet food but eat this in the middle of a workday? Naptime here I come!

This is just one of those places where the members usually ordered off the menu. At the same time, their guests ate the fatten lathe menu selections and became sedated. Unless guests are "in the know" or your lunch date ordered first, guests are stuck with what's listed on the piece of parchment.

On to lesson number two: in Bob's rules of business, for all business gatherings, if possible, have the meeting on your home field. If you can't have a home-field advantage, then find some neutral ground. Always avoid going to the other person's office. It puts you at a disadvantage. He also taught me that even casual lunches and get-togethers were still business meetings. I should treat them as such. Most importantly, his number one rule: don't waste people's time.

I hadn't worked for Bob for in a while, so while he talked about his kid's all-star baseball team, I tried to figure out my next move. Now don't get me wrong. I am not a harsh person who could care less about his kids. I just knew boasting about his child's sports accomplishments is not his main reason for having lunch with me. I had learned a lot from the man sitting across from me, and I figured the best thing to do is cut to the chase, or we'd be eating lunch all day.

Just as I opened my mouth to speak, the waiter showed up.

"Ah, Mr. Carlson, how very nice to see you again," he blathered. This guy had the fakest smile I had ever seen. "Will it be the usual?" he inquired while showing his fangs.

"Not today, James," Bob answered. The waiter beamed when Bob addressed him by name. "Do me a favor, James, would you? See if Lance will make me up a Caesar salad, no croutons, with an ice tea. And you, Max?"

"I'll have the same," I answered. It is easier than making a decision.

The waiter acknowledged and left. I waited for a bow too, but I guess that went out in the '80s. "So, Bob, to what do I owe this pleasure?" I put on my best, "I know what you are up to smile."

He grinned back at me and then leaned forward to rest his chin in his hands. "You know, Max, you were always one of my favorite employees. Bright, articulate…."

"Opinionated and stubborn, too," I added.

"And modest. Anyway, I knew you'd outgrow us sooner or later…" Bob reached under the table and pulled an envelope from his briefcase. He placed it in the space between us. "And, of course, you did well for yourself."

"Yep," I said. "I've done okay."

"So has your company. I've been watching your publication for some time now. It looks like you've managed to increase your market coverage along with your revenues without increasing expenses at the same time. Amazingly, you haven't encountered a downside. That's some trick." Could he have been paying attention more than I'd given him credit?

"I'll get to the point, Maxi. Corporate has bestowed a pile of money on me, allowing me to invest in similar businesses that may mesh Well, with our little media company." Now the conversation is getting interesting. "Bottom line, Maxi, I want to buy out *The Guide*."

"You want to buy my company?" I am surprised. This is not what I expected. Well, I hoped for an ego stroke like a high-level job offer, but this? W.O.W., selling *The Guide* would solve so many problems. I could buy Jon off. I could do something different. I could start over someplace else. My hand hit my forehead. No, I couldn't because Ric would not want to leave Mayberry. But still…

Bob ignored my head slap and slid the large envelope across the table. "Maxi, take a look at my offer. It is for the whole chain, including your out of market publications too. Have your lawyer call my office once you check it out. As part of the deal, I'd like you to stay on for a year after the sale and advise us on profitability directions. You seem to excel at that. Plus, you wouldn't be on the staff. You wouldn't need to put up with any of the bullshit that goes on." He waved his hand with the statement.

I had underestimated Bob. He did know what went on in his building.

"After that, if you want, I would find a place in the organization for you. Don't give me an answer now." He held up both hands. "Just think about it."

"Okay, I will." Where the heck did that voice come from? Sometimes I even surprised myself.

Our salads arrived, and the small talk resumed. I wished I could sneak off to the Ladies Room and peek into the envelope, but I thought Bob would notice. I just wanted to know if the offer is an "oh my God" or a "you've got to be kidding" number.

Lunch dragged on until finally, Bob looked at his watch and simultaneously signaled for the check. I had eaten about half my salad although I don't think I had tasted any of it.

"Thanks again for your time, Maxi. There is a short deadline for this. You know headquarters."

That statement got the old eye roll.

"If I don't come up with a plan, they'll shift funds to another market. *The Guide* is just one of several publications under consideration. Will Friday work for a follow-up?"

I shook my head yes and leaned in to give Bob a corporate hug, a gesture where one circles the other with their arms and squeezes gently. If I were male, it would be the equivalent of a pat on the back. I wanted to sprint to my car, rip open the envelope, and scream or cry aloud, but he watched me as I walked away. I knew if I showed any enthusiasm, I would blow any negotiation room I might need later. Bob taught me well.

I turned and waved, opened my car door, and slid into the driver's seat. I then ripped the envelope open before I placed my pocketbook on the passenger's side. "Dear Ms. Malloni-Jacobs, As publisher of *The Guide*, blah, blah, blah . . ." Where is the good stuff? Holy crap! I put my hand over my mouth and stared at the dollar amount: five million dollars cash plus an additional two hundred thousand to stay on for the first year. "Wow." I sat back to gape at the numbers, quickly calculating after the legal fees and a considerable bonus for Nancy I would still clear a lot of money. Enough money to start over big time!

I might still have to give half to Jon, who didn't deserve jack, but I bet he'd get off my back quickly with even a small pile of cash! Why had I let this divorce drag on?

"Thank you, Bob!" I yelled as I pulled my car back towards the shore. I needed to talk with Nancy and get these papers over to Gert. This had to be as enjoyable as winning Lotto!

Chapter Six

Nancy sat at her desk, phone in hand. I pulled up one of the lobby chairs, sat down across from her, and placed the envelope on her desk close to me, just like Bob Carlson had done in the restaurant. Nancy raised one eyebrow and continued her conversation. To someone who didn't know better, one would think we were in Nancy's office, and I am her employee. I start to bounce in the chair until she finally wraps up the call.

"What?" she snaps at me, still eyeing the envelope.

"How'd ya like to make six figures, the easy way?" I slid the envelope towards her.

Nancy peeked in and smiled. "I had a feeling," she began to read the offer. "So…."

"So, what?"

"So, I didn't know we were for sale. Did you decide already what you are going to do?" She leaned back in her chair and crossed her arms.

"I haven't decided yet. Bob gave me until Friday to respond." I shifted in the chair and leaned in closer to Nancy's desk. "It's a real decent offer, and it would get me out of part of the mess I'm in."

Nancy nodded. If anyone, besides me, experienced the brunt of my break-up, it was Nancy.

Between the court dates and my after-court-date breakdowns, she kept everything going. Nancy is a huge asset in building the business. I wondered if I could get her a temp gig with Bob too. She had just as much stake in my decision as I did.

"You'll need to give the slime-ex a share unless you are divorced before the sale goes through," Nancy pointed out.

"That already occurred to me. Jon is being a creep about my money, so this is a way to buy him off. I'll need to check with Gert."

She rolled her eyes. "You may want to have someone else take a look too, Max."

And then it's my turn to do the eye roll. I slid the envelope back in her direction.

"After all, we are talking about a major deal. If this was surgery, you'd get a second opinion, right?"

I hated it when she did this, but again, Nancy had the right approach. "Maybe. Would you send a copy over to Gert for me? I'll let her know it's on the way."

"By the way, now that we're on the subject of lawyers. I think you need to hire someone in Newport just in case the situation becomes political."

"Can't Gert take care of this too?" The standard procedure for anything legal for the last two years is first it went to Gert than she decided if it needed to be farmed out.

"Fine." I watched Nancy toss the envelope containing our future on top of a stack of papers. She scribbled something on a piece of paper while I got up to go into my office. I looked back at the pile. I never understood Nancy's filing system.

After the initial buzz of the deal faded, I am not sure how I felt about giving up my little company to the big corporation in the city. I see firsthand how they gobble up their competition. Their new acquisition stumbles and fails because of the bureaucracy within the company. Did I want to take a chance with something I worked so hard to build? I knew business is supposed to be non-emotional, but with me, it's hard not to look at my business as a second child.

"It's just business, Max, get over it." I moved towards my desk, shuffled through the stack of messages, and quickly decided not to answer any. All I could think about is how great it would be if this all worked out. I could get rid of Jon, keep Ric, and get that little condominium by the marina. I could start another company — something fun — like an ice cream parlor or a video game arcade or a live music venue for teenagers.

Ric would be happy because we would be staying in town. Jon would be happy — not that it mattered — because he'd have a massive pile of cash from my sweat equity.   And me? Would this finally make me happy? I need to add a psychic to my staff.

I went back to shuffling through my messages. Here is one from my old Newport rep. Hmmm, interesting. Puzzo's Restaurant had called. Maybe the family finally decided they needed to advertise. My mom had called. I put that one in my briefcase. I need to remember to call her back.

But the message I waited for wasn't there. Zack said it wouldn't be another twenty years, and I knew in guy time three days is nothing, but in girl time, it is an eternity. Maybe this is a good thing. He isn't part of my destiny, and karma threw him away early on before I got too attached. I looked out to the seagrass for an answer.

"Maxi, what are you doing?" Out of the corner of my eye, I could see Nancy leaning in my doorway.

"Nothing," I replied, still watching the grass.

"Well,, go home and do that." Nancy crossed the room in two strides. She slammed down my briefcase and instructed, "You're disrupting my sense of mayhem."

"Sorry." I got up and walked towards the door, leaving everything on my desk. "I think you're right. There is too much on my mind. I'd better go home and think about it."

"Don't forget to call your mother," she reminded. I waved and got into my car. There were some things one could only find in a shoreline town. Nosy neighbors and gossip hounds were everywhere. So were fine restaurants. Only in a summer community could one buy homemade ice cream while looking out over the Connecticut River and Long Island Sound. I pulled out of the driveway and headed left towards the point, making sure to check my speed. Another thing common in small shoreline towns were speed traps along the routes to all the pretty spots.

I cruise down the tree-lined Main Street, enjoying the busyness of people. The air is hot, humid, and heavy. I found a parking space at the point up front, right where I could see the lighthouse, boats, mini-golf, and people from my air-conditioned car. I stand in line to get ice cream, while sailboats cruise by, the smell of fried clams lingers, and a slight breeze off the water.

"Mint chip, please," The teenager handed me my cone. I over-tipped. I couldn't wait for Ric to get one of these summer jobs, so I would get free ice cream. The owner used this benefit to recruit new hires. YUM! I walked over to a railing and watched some kids throwing bread into the water for the seagulls. The sun melted my face, and my shoulder muscles loosened. Mint chip ice cream always does my body right.

I pulled my cell phone out of my pocket and hit auto-dial for my mom. The phone rang twice before I heard my father's voice.

"Hello." His smile slipped through the line.

"Hey, Dad, is Mom around? She called me earlier."

"Nope. She went to the store."

I could picture my dad sitting in his recliner, watching a classic football game on ESPN, or something on late afternoon TV, or I just woke him from his daily nap.

"Well,, let her know I called back, OK?" I unconsciously walked back towards my car.

"No problem. What else is going on?"

"Not much." It's not that I didn't want to tell him the news of the possible sale. I didn't think I needed or wanted his advice yet. This is something I need to work out for myself. Of course, once I decided I'd ask him what he thought, and after hearing his advice, I might change my mind. I always respected his opinion, even if I didn't always take his advice.

"Alright, I'll tell Mom you called."

I got into my overheated car and drove over to Ed's Grocery, located in the only shopping plaza in town off Route 1. The original Ed died years ago, and his grandson, Ed, the third or fourth, I can never remember which ran the place. I had to time my visits very carefully because the entire town, including Jon and his future wife, shopped here. Ed's just one of the many "Mayberry" things that went on here.

I looked over the list I had put together while waiting for the light to change. Peppers, hamburger, rice, onion soup mix, tomato soup, Italian bread, and bag o'salad. I would figure ten minutes tops if I didn't stop and chat. Considering I am currently the top gossip topic, it would be hard to avoid the conversations of the curious. I timed my visit in between the stay-at-home moms who blame my husband's wandering on me choosing to work, and the other worker bees, most of whom believe the tart did me a favor. They thought I should get myself a trophy husband who would work for a living so I could take a break.

My problem had always been I am more attracted to rock guitarists than corporate VP's. What can I say? If a guy can hold a guitar, then in my mind, he's sexy. I also had always had a unique ability to find the only handsome guy in the room, at least to me, with the lowest paying job. Love came in there somewhere while lust made an appearance pretty fast. I guess being the responsible one made me cynical.

I waited patiently for the light to change, and it occurred to me that only I would want to cook something in the oven on a ninety-degree day. Oh Well,, this is why air conditioning was invented.

The parking Gods are with me, and I began to think the whole dinner thing is my own form of manifest destiny. Someone came up with the idea of having fresh watermelons iced on the sidewalk in huge barrel type coolers. One still had ice, and the rest were sweating, creating huge puddles by the door. What was once fresh watermelons looked like mush.

Great marketing idea, I thought, after entering the store and getting such a blast of frigid air. I just might freeze to death before I finish getting my groceries. If they combined the two concepts, Ed could sell semi-frozen watermelons to go. I bet the tourists would buy them up if he advertised the frozen watermelons as a local favorite.

I grabbed a basket to begin my quest for a nice dinner. My plan is to hit the produce section first, then work my way through the store and hit the bakery last. I noticed a few familiar faces. I smiled and nodded to Ric's friend's mother, whose name I could never remember. She's inspecting the grapes in the next aisle. After finding two fresh green peppers and throwing them into the basket, I scooped up a bag of lettuce, pre-washed and chopped, so I wouldn't have to do it myself. In the soup aisle, I grabbed a box of instant onion soup and two cans of Campbell's tomato soup. My basket is getting a bit heavy as I backtrack to the meat section. And my luck runs out.

"Well,, her husband left her. It's his choice. I can't help it if he's that stupid. I just happened to be, ya know, there. I don't see why people are making all those, you know, judgments."

It could only be the squeaky voice of the Tart. I peeked around the corner, and there she stood wearing high heels, a halter top, and short shorts. She looked like a stripper on break in between shows. She held her cell phone to her ear, facing away from me, and talked away.

"I don't care what she does. Listen, I know it's not much longer, and this is the plan, sort of. I don't like it, and I am tired of it. It's been going on way too long. I want my life normal again."

Her voice got a little high pitched. That woman could whine.

"Well,, whatever you do, just keep her away from me and finish this quick."

Silence. She stopped and reached for a ketchup bottle, taking the time to read the ingredients before putting it back on the shelf. Oh, give me a break! Like she cared what's in ketchup!

"Fine. I said, fine. I just don't understand why…"

I wish I could hear the other side of her conversation. It sounded interesting.

"I'm bored. Isn't that enough? Okay, sis, I get it. I gotta go."

Hillsey snapped her cell phone shut, tossed it into her open purse, and moved around the corner swaying her hips like she is on the prowl for another good time. I walked over to the meat counter and got my hamburger, then focused on hitting the bakery without being seen. I had illusions of Lady Luck back with me until I reached the check-out, and there stood Hillsey in all her glory, flirting with Ed the fourth. She bent forward, and Ed leaned in with his head making it obvious he's peeking down her shirt to get a gander at the goods.

Just behind the Tart, Toni, Randi, and Lucy, three of the baseball moms, strolled in. This trio fell into the stay-at-home category. They spent their days reflecting on how their perfect kids perform in academics, sports, and other hobbies as a way of elevating their status as perfect parents. At the Little League games, they sat in the stands and complained about the coaches, umpires, and anyone else who make life seem unfair for their perfect offspring.

This is perfect timing on their part. Lucy glimpsed over and waved. I faked a smile and raised my hand while still trying to go unnoticed. Then, Lucy caught Hillsey's eye. She knows this woman could not possibly be waving at her because she slowly turned and glared in my direction. The surprised look on her face told anyone close by I am the last person she wants to see. If looks could kill, I would be a pile of ashes.

"Hey Max," Toni called out as the three giggles, then scoot towards produce. I see them stacked above one another as they peek around the corner. I could imagine the conversation as they lay about doing nothing on the town beach tomorrow: "And Maxi glared at Hillsey. Hillsey gave her a dirty look back. Them Maxi said something, and Hillsey said something back. The two of them started wrestling right there in the middle of the supermarket. Can you believe it? I mean, come on, like Jon is worth all this!" Then the giggles would start.

Hillsey and I gave each other the stare down. All I want to do is to make some sweet stuffed peppers. I turned back to the cashier, who had my order rung up, shove a twenty into her hand, grabbed my groceries, and without waiting for my change, head towards the door. My face a beautiful shade of crimson, as I thought instead of pepper stuffing, I would rather stuff Hillsey into the meat grinder.

My heel hit the sidewalk, and I skid, falling on my behind just shy of the parking lot. Apparently, someone, probably the same person who came up with the watermelons on ice idea, thought it would be a plus to drain the barrels of the water. This rocket scientist failed to move the rubber mats from the entrance, so they became slippery once the water and melon slime spread over them.

A young man in an Ed's bib headed towards me. I pushed myself up, held onto my grocery bag in one hand, and limped to my car. As I unlocked my door, I glanced back at my reflection in the store window and saw the back of my skirt isn't only wet, it's also covered in green slime. Not exactly perfect for my cloth seats.

In front of me sat a bright yellow VW Bug convertible with the bumper sticker: I Brake for Unicorns & Millionaires. Hillsey's car. This has fun potential. I could hop out and key it. No even better, I could bump it into traffic. Or I could call Triple-A and have it towed. Of course, I'd need to get a bit more creative on the reason. Huh. I could consider slashing the tires or pouring soda across the hood. I could run back into Ed's and buy a raw fish. Oh, I know, I could go pick up Alfred, the town drunk, and pay him to pee all over the car.

I started to giggle. If I pre-planned this encounter, I would have brought a present from my neighbor's ninety-pound lab in my trunk. I could just leave the everyday brown bag under her front seat to simmer. I shook my head, checked behind me, and backed out. At times, revenge is better planned than executed. In my mind, this almost made me a better person.

Chapter Seven

Ric would be home from camp in a half hour. I took a quick shower, changed into shorts and a tank top. I flung my stained dress and shoes out the bathroom window. I will need to remember to put them in the garbage can. Part of me wants to castrate Ed for his stupidity, and the other part just wants to forget and go back to my happy mood. According to my horoscope, I would soon be getting a surprise. I figure the karma gods were running a few days late since Zack had shown up. Maybe the surprise would be a call to go out again.

Since I hadn't put the paper in the recycling bin this morning, I opened it to re-read the horoscope. "Today will be full of surprises as your past meets your present." And my interpretation is a guy would do the surprising. Still, now I'm awake and reading, I suppose it could be anything. Damn.

I got the rice going, and while it cooked, I cleaned the peppers, cut them in two, then arranged the four pieces in a white ceramic soufflé dish — one of the many shower gifts from way back when I was stupid and in love. This was the highlight of the pre-wedding festivities for Jon. He fussed over everything we got. "Babe, free shit," he repeated. He was amazing back then. I thought I had it made, although I have to admit, I had my doubts we would be getting married if I wasn't pregnant. He was much more mellow than I would ever be and liked living by the seat of his pants. I, on the other hand, like a little more stability.

We were destined for disaster from the beginning.

I mixed the raw hamburger and onion soup thoroughly and added the rice once it finished cooking. Carefully I stuffed this mixture into each pepper. I opened the Campbell's tomato soup and spread it across the top. After I rinsed out the can, I poured the side goop into the dish too.

"Voila!" I exclaim, feeling pretty proud of myself, as Ric came up the walk. Man, is he ever going to be surprised! The porch door slammed as I reached for the soufflé pan and lifted it to the edge of the counter.

"Hey, Mom!" Ric shouted, arriving home dirty and sweaty from a full day at camp.

I put a smile on and turned. Somehow in the process of turning the pan slipped out of my hand and crashed to the floor. We both stared in disbelief. "Shit," I yelled. "Shit, shit, shit."

"Mom, do you…" My hand went up to shush him. He exited quickly. I could see the top of his head when his eyes peeked around the corner, checking to see whether I am going into a complete or partial meltdown.

"Shit. Shit. Shit." I ran my left hand through my hair and stared at the mess. I started to babble. "All I wanted to do is make a nice dinner, sit with my son, and eat like a normal family. Nothing fancy, just…

Then the Tart and the townie baseball moms and the watermelon and...."

"Mom, I'll help clean up." Ric crept slowly back into the kitchen.

"No," I said way too loud. "And I would leave if I were you." Ric ran out of the room. His sneakers pounded up the stairs.

Tomato soup, raw hamburger, rice, peppers, and broken glass lay at my feet in front of my stove. Tomato soup splattered across the room on my fridge, walls, and table. Even the dead herb plants Jon said were supposed to be a fresh herb garden had glop. I knew staring at the mess wasn't going to clean it. Times like this, I missed Jon. He would put his arm around me and told me to go take a shower because I had tomato soup glop all over me too. He would talk to me in that soothing voice, walk me out of the kitchen, and move me towards the stairs, knowing I am on the verge of tears. By the time I finished cleaning myself up, the kitchen would be clean, and he probably would find a take-out place that made stuffed peppers. If only Jon were there.

I slapped myself hard on the side of my head. "Dammit!" The tears started. I began to pick up the peppers to toss them into the trash. I reach over a piece of a broken dish. "Ouch!" The acid from the tomato sunk in the cut on my finger. It stung like crazy. I watch my blood combine with the tomato soup. My stomach cramped.

I head for the bathroom, run water over my finger, grab a Band-Aid, and wonder how I am going to clean up the mess with a cut on my finger. I checked under my kitchen sink, only to find silver polish for silver I don't own, starch for shirts I will never iron, brass cleaner, and… Behind the brass cleaner, I found a pair of rubber gloves—dishwashing gloves to be exact. I don't know how they got here. I clean up the stuff on my floor. I spray down the walls and the fridge, the herb table, and everyplace else I find red glop. I took the garbage bag out to the trash, joining my dress and shoes as a display of the day.

"Phase one is complete," Next stop, the upstairs bathroom. I could hear Ric's fingers tapping away inside his room. I guess he's playing a video game. Quickly I wash, dress, and get ready to go out to find dinner for Ric and I. I emerged to hear Ric downstairs talking to someone, and I smelled pizza.

"Hey!" I said. "You didn't!" The tears started. Ric stood next to the kitchen table, holding a pizza box.

"Half spinach, half pineapple," he beamed. Gosh, my kid had a knock-out smile. In a few years, all the little girls would be calling. I cried harder. "Mom, I thought I was helping…"

"You are babe, you are. I'm just…" Ric got plates out. I could see by the way he moved, he wanted to be somewhere else. "Ric, this is perfect. Thank you."

We parked ourselves at the kitchen table, dove into the tomato cheesy pineapple treat, and started to tell the tales of our day.

Chapter Eight

There is nothing more spectacular than the sun rising over a calm ocean. I don't witness this often enough. This morning I got up at five-thirty, walked to the beach, sat in the sand, and enjoyed the beautiful glow. I am now at peace with the world.

After having all the planets align correctly, I managed to leave the house on time. Then Murphy's Law struck. My horoscope warned me not to get too comfortable. Man, horoscopes are scary some days. I turned my car on to I-95. I hear the tell-tale ring tone.

"What!" I had been in traffic for fifteen minutes without moving an inch, getting later for an appointment with the evil twins, Dickhead and Dimwad, over at Gert's office. Nancy called. Casey, my old Newport rep, the one who had left and started a competing publication, had forgotten to distribute five thousand copies of the last guide. She just "found" them in her storage space and wanted to know what she should do with them. I had a few choice ideas. I kept them to myself and just asked if our distribution guy could pick them up. If this was the last issue, we could still get them out on the stands.

"Oh, and Maxi, one of our Boston reps, just quit too." I let out a slight yelp. If one more thing goes wrong, I swore I would turn my car around and head south toward Key West. Once there, I'd do what an old college friend threatened — blow up the seven-mile bridge so no one could come after me. I'd live out the rest of my life sitting on a beach, drinking margaritas, and never even considering going back to reality. My life would be an endless Jimmy Buffet song.

I hung up. My cell rang. Now it's Gert's turn. "What else is wrong?"

"Maxi, darling, breathe." Gert's calming voice came through my cheap cell phone. She sounded like one of those relaxation tapes that had been copied too many times, all static and breathy. "You sound like you're about to go over the edge. He's not worth it."

I listened and inhaled a long, deep breath. I should tell her this is not about Jon. "Gert, I'm on 95 on the way to your office, and traffic is not moving. I think I'm going to be late."

"So be late. So am I," she chimed back. "I need to file a motion, and I am waiting for the judge to come back. I'll get there as soon as I can. The evil twins will just have to wait."

"Ha. If traffic moves, oh, wait, we are moving. Finally!" I blew out another sigh as my car crept along, finally coming over the top of a hill, so I could see what the holdup is. "There's nothing there!" I screamed. "These idiots on 95 slow down for nothing. I can't stand this!"

"Maxi, do as I say. Breathe!" Gert, thank heavens, interrupted what could have gone on indefinitely. "Meet me at the office. I'm being called back into court now. I will be there as soon as I can. Do not, I repeat, do not attempt to negotiate with the butt heads. I am a professional. Let me do it."

"Gert, I can negotiate," I sounded whiney. I hated it when she took cheap shots. She knew I had sold guides in all those markets across four states, worked with several major corporations for ad dollars, and put together my own print contracts. I knew how to negotiate.

"I know you do, darling. It's just you conduct your guide negotiations in non-emotional situations. I, however, negotiate in highly emotional situations. You're nice. I have ice in my veins and can be a royal bitch. I repeat again, do not attempt a negotiation until I get there. Promise?"

"I promise. See you at the office." I clicked off the phone and tried to concentrate on driving, although driving is the last thing on my mind. I told myself to think positive, and this would all be over soon. If I only believed my mantra.

If I thought about my life, I was self-loathing in hell. I had the divorce thing going on, hopefully not much longer, though I knew better. Jon wanted something besides the boat, and he would use Ric to get it. It wasn't money; I was quite sure he had money squirreled away somewhere. After all, I had been paying all the bills since the beginning. If he was broke, where did all his cash go? Probably buying jewels for Hillsey. Yeah, right. My hand hit the side of my head. Like he even needed to buy her jewelry to get laid.

I took in another cleansing breath, filling my stomach with as much air as physically possible. I slowly let it flow out my nose.

I wish I could figure out what Jon wanted from me. The meetings between him and our lawyers made me a nervous wreck. I didn't like stepping into the unknown. I also knew when you swim in toilets, you're bound to get surrounded by crap. And it felt like I am SCUBA diving into sewers.

I would give him everything if he would just give up on Ric. Gert said that attitude was going to get me in trouble, and we needed to be tough and go for his balls. That's why I hired her. She aggravated the hell out of Jon. Since the day I brought her on to handle the business legal stuff, Jon had been on my back to fire her. He used to get angry whenever I gave her another project. "You don't know this woman," he'd say. "She could be ripping you off. Over-charging you. Who knows, Maxi?" Then the best part would come, "I just don't like to see people take advantage of you, Max."

The bizarre part was Jon loved anybody who would do his work. He rarely had an unkind word to say. Yet where Gert is concerned, Jon spit poison. After she sued an old employee because he filed for unemployment benefits he didn't deserve, Jon wanted to fire her. He said she had wasted more of my money than he did. He got to fire someone: me. Or I fired him. Either way, it all worked out.

I took a quick turn off the exit, into Gert's driveway. My lawyer's office is one big illusion. She moved into an old Victorian last year. The building is surrounded by wildflower gardens, the outside feminine, warm, and inviting. Her conference room another world, more like her, strong, unique, and all business. Sitting in the power seat, as Gert liked to call the home side of the mahogany conference table, her clients looked out onto the gardens, a view Gert hoped provided peace and perspective. I remember when she first moved in.

"The view is going to give my clients a sense of inner peace, while the adversaries look at my awesome credentials, and feel intimidated by my mere presence," she laughed.

Typical Gert. On the light paneled conference wall, she hung her degrees, along with a few custom-framed headlines from high profile cases she had won, and a metal sculpture if you examined carefully you would see she had a squished frog in the center. "Adversaries are lower than pond scum." Gert's motto. The sculpture is there to make them feel at home. Most visiting lawyers didn't get it, and, in several meetings, they actually complimented Gert on her taste in art. Go figure.

She took the analogy a step further. Amongst the leather-bound books surround the TV/VCR cabinet, they were smaller ceramic frogs. At that moment, I wanted to take a frog or two and to shove it up my ex and his sleazy lawyer's butt. I watched as the overpaid sleaze bag whispered something into Jon's ear. Jon showed his oily smile, so I knew he is probably plotting another way to screw me, if not then a crude recount of a woman who stooped to date him. Either way, they creeped me out.

What did I ever see in this anorexic, greasy-haired, slimeball? I just didn't get it. Maybe I was high on the music, or someone had put acid in my water at a show. At least I got Ric, who is adorable and took after me as far as morals, values, and looks. I kept looking out the window over their shoulders, hoping to see

Gert's car pull in. The wildflowers created a rainbow of color around the windowpane. It is quite beautiful. Jon's lawyer's eye and mine met. Crap. Now he is smiling at me.

"Maxi, let's talk." He rested his chin on his hands in a lame attempt to look innocent.

"I have nothing to talk to you about," I held both arms across my chest and leaned away. Check out my body language, buddy. How much more disgusted could I look?

"Come on, Max," Jon moaned. "You and I could settle this. I just want what's fair. You know. I would never take advantage of you."

"Really? You never wanted to take advantage of me? I guess that's why you left Ric and me, huh? Figured it was best for… for who, Jon?" I hit myself on the side of my head. "Best for you, perhaps? Well, since you said that, alright, what do you really want, Jon? Why am I here?" I could hear Gert's voice screaming in my head; do not attempt any negotiating without me. Well,, Gert's not here, so . . .

"I'm going to tape this," Jon's lawyer piped in as he placed a small cassette player on the table. "We don't want any misinterpretations in the future, do we?" He grinned, without teeth. He looked scary. I resolved I would bury this dude.

"I agree." I also smiled without teeth. "We wouldn't want anything misinterpreted. Now, Jon," even saying his name politely took effort, "what do you want?"

"Don't answer." Gert burst into the room like a tornado on fire. Dressed in a bright red power suit, I feel her hand hit me in the back of the head.

"Hey!"

"What did I tell you?" Her face inches from mine as she slid into the chair next to me.

"But, Gert..."

"No buts. What did I tell you? No talking without me." Gert opened up her briefcase and peered over at Jon and Luke, ready to pounce. "Gentlemen, let us begin. You called this meeting, so let's hear what you have to say."

Luke adjusted himself in his seat and then poured on his oily smile. "I agree, let's begin." He appeared to undress Gert with his eyes. Not a good idea. She could bite him. "My client wants to get everything settled to give his son a more balanced household situation. We are proposing since Mr. Jacobs has a stable environment with his two future stepchildren living with him and his fiancée, Ric moves in with Mr. Jacobs and his future bride until further notice."

"Over my dead—OW!!!" Gert's heel drove into my foot.

"No," Gert answered stoically. Her face was frozen with no emotion.

"Excuse me?"

"I said no. You know, as well, as I do, no court in the country is going to give Mr. Jacobs custody. He abandoned his wife and child and then proceeded to an extramarital affair. We've already had this conversation, counselor, and the answer is still no." Gert adjusted herself to sit forward on her chair, my gaze moved from her eyes to his, as they engaged in a staring contest. As though whoever flinched first lost.

"Then we need to settle the divorce proceedings now. Court time is Monday at ten. We need the child in a stable routine. That routine includes all recreational activities he took advantage of when Mr. and Mrs. Jacobs were together. My client is willing to be second under the condition he retains visitation rights, boat rights, and ongoing financial benefits from half-ownership in Mrs. Jacobs' business. That way, Mr. Jacobs can maintain a similar environment to what the child will have while residing with Mrs. Jacobs. I filed this recommendation with the court, a recommendation is in the best interests of the child." Luke sat back and crossed his arms in triumph. He and Jon glanced at each other, confidence oozing from their side of the table.

Gert closed her eyes, not saying a word. "It's not going to happen," she stated calmly. "First, as mentioned before, you can't have custody, only visitation rights. Second, if this is about the boat and business, don't drag the child into it. That's just low." Gert took in a deep breath. I noticed both Jon and Luke watch her breasts rise. "And third, you don't deserve any part of Maxi's business, and you know it. Records show you haven't earned any unless there is something that is showing you do. As far as the boat goes, Well, here we have an argument. What shall we do?"

I started to speak, but Gert dug her nails into my thigh.

"I think we should sell the boat and split the proceeds. If Mrs. Jacobs wants to retain the vessel, she needs to pay Mr. Jacobs half of its replacement value."

"Current value," Gert instructed.

Jon leaned over and whispered something in Luke's ear. "Will that move us along?" he inquired. In all this time, he hadn't taken his eyes off Gert. That poor woman is going to need a shower.

"Yes." Gert and Luke went back to their staring contest. Was it my imagination? I thought I saw a flicker that suggested more is going on. Could it be passion? Probably more anger than desire. There is a thin line between love and hate.

"I guess we have a date for Monday," Luke said as he reached across the table and shook Gert's hand. I withdraw mine before he could touch it, not wanting to catch anything. "Oh, and Mrs. Jacobs, please remember my client gets to spend this weekend with his son. Friday from five in the evening until Sunday at five in the evening. I will go with the assumption you will abide."

I put on my tough girl face and gave them the chin nod, watching as both shuffled out the door. "Gert, I'm…"

Gert's hand went up. I stopped talking. I learned long ago when she is pissed, I should just shut up. I waited for the explosion.

"So, how was your date?" She changed the subject and spoke calmly.

"OK."

"You should go on more of those." Gert started shuffling papers at the table. Her gaze drifted out the window.

"Yeah." I shifted my weight from the right side to left uncomfortably. "Uh, Gert, what just went on here?"

"He wants the boat and cash. Ric is secondary. We just agreed to give him half the value of the boat in cash." I felt tears in my eyes as Gert kept going. "I don't know what they are up to, but I think we should go to court Monday and find out. In the meantime, you should take off this weekend and go to a spa or something. Don't sit home alone without Ric. Not good karmically..." She sat back down. I took a long look. Her hair is less than perfect. There were slight wrinkles in her suit, and oh my, were those bags under her eyes? It is not like Gert to be disheveled.

"Are you OK?" I asked while brushing her arm with my hand.

"Yeah, I'm fine," she sighed. "Just getting a little tired of all this, that's all. I think I need a vacation. Some change. Anyway, Max, lets fight this one on Monday, and don't worry, I'll take care of it."

Feeling dismissed, I forced a smile and headed out to my car, swallowing hard to control the tears that wanted to seep out. In the distance, the noon siren from the fire department sounded. I should go to work. I had a lot to do but no motivation. What I needed now is weekend plans or a nap. Either one would do the trick. I think I'll take a ride to the marina and rest on the Sludge Puppy. I'd take it out if I could dock it myself, but I am not talented. It would be nice to anchor in the sound and rock softly with the rhythm of the water. Maybe Molly could help me dock. I pulled out onto Rte. 1 and turned on my cell phone only to discover a few messages.

As I navigated through the traffic, I had no desire to talk to anyone. I could picture the water glistening with sunshine. I made another executive decision. I am going to sit, sulk, and nap aboard MY boat while I still could. Gosh, I'd never been so irresponsible in my life. I wondered how much longer I'd have the authority to make such decisions. Bob Carlson would probably want me in the office from eight in the morning until six at night five days a week. Just the thought made me cringe.

Chapter Nine

The drive from Gert's office to the marina is just short enough for my responsible Virgo personality to kick in. I returned all but one phone message. BY accomplishing something, I justified a stop at Ashley's for lemon pie ice cream.

Ashley's is a little wooden shack on the side of US 1 next to a clam bar and a marina. They claim to be open all year, but once the weather turns and the wind begins to howl across the water, "open" is a general term. When they get back on a regular schedule, the locals celebrate.

My last phone call troubled me; Bob Carlson's secretary gave a reminder about Friday. He said something about dollars available, and he needed to tweak his budget to accommodate this buy. Bob seemed more like the schmoozer type who left the deal-making to others. Did I underestimate his abilities?

Making the deadline an actual deadline complicates things. I thought I could avoid making a decision until the following week. Now Nancy needs to get the paperwork over to Gert ASAP. She had "forgotten" to send it because little emergencies kept coming up. I got pissed off, then cut her slack. Nancy had always been loyal to me. Heck, last winter, Nancy drove up to Burlington Vermont in a snowstorm to attend a meeting of all the ski resorts. She insisted this is our business, and we needed to be there.

After Gert checked out the proposal, I would need to get Nancy's real opinion, not that she ever hesitates to give that out. She had always had a considerable say in decisions because I trust her. This is the sign it's time to run the offer past my dad too.

"Crap." I bang my hand against the steering wheel in annoyance. I didn't need another decision on my plate. I just gave up my boat, for crying aloud.

I'd had vivid dreams lately, probably related to my date with Zack, but I wasn't sure. Zack, along with other actual exes, had been the stars in a kind of 'what if' scenario. The type of dream that makes you second-guess your life choices. For me, these dreams tend to happen when my reality falls apart. Last night had been intense and brought back memories I thought I'd let go but apparently just buried away.

The dream took me back to my eighth-grade picnic when the school took us out to a Y camp in town. The camp was cool with swimming, volleyball, horseshoes, hiking paths, a ball field, and such. My kid would think a place like this is lame since it didn't have a rock-climbing wall, computer lab, or laser tag. However, in the late seventies, the Y camp is the place to be.

The weird part about Zack and me is we had moments together that never stuck. What actually happened at this picnic was my friends, obnoxious pre-teen girls, much like myself, decided we needed a picture of the two of us. One took my hand, and the

86

other took his and pulled our hands together. Zack put his arm around me, and we stood there in bathing suits smiling. I still had the picture somewhere. It was the most electrifying moment with Zack in my life until the kiss he gave me at the restaurant. I could feel the warmth and weight of his arm on my shoulder for days afterward. They took the picture, and then I giggled, blushed, and walked away on cloud nine while he went back with his buds.

Innocent times. My dream, not so much. Same picture same situation, except in my dream Zack whispers in my ear, "Let's go for a hike."

"OK," I allow him to lead me away while whoops and hollering filled the background. Of course, it's just the two of us in the woods. The chaperones were missing. No other kids came down the trail.

I'd always loved the forests in New England. Shades of greens and browns with sun rays peeking through the leaves. We walked along with the well-traveled path a-ways. Zack took me in his arms. "I've wanted to do this all year," he whispers. I'm nervous and shaking. I mean, come on! I am only thirteen! He leans his face towards mine and then…my freaking alarm goes off to drag me back to my pathetic reality!

I try going back to sleep, but the moment, like my past, disappears.

Maybe I am using Zack as a diversion from my reality. It's not like he'd called since our dinner date. Not that I expected he would.

No. I take that back. I more than expected it. I thought we'd have at least a phone conversation a day. At night I became an awkward adolescent, and during the day, he popped into my brain at the strangest times.

I turned back into obsessive Maxi, wondering what he is doing or, better yet, whom he's doing it with. How did this happen? I could remember that being the big question the summer between junior high and high school. Every party I didn't go to of course he did. The only question I would ask, "Was he with anybody?"

He never was, at least according to my friends. They might be lying. People do that to protect people they care about. When Jon first started to date the Tart, they were pretty much out in the open about it. He would meet her at The Farm, a local dive in town. From what I heard, they would drink a few beers, play pool, and do things he and I would do before we had Ric.

I found out after Jon left several of "my friends" had known about the Tart since the beginning. They didn't feel their place to tell me.

"You're my freaking friends!" I shouted when I discovered they knew. Of course, I had to find out at a Memorial Day picnic at one of their houses. After we started to get buzzed on Mike's Lemonades, it all came out. I acted like a total adult. After refusing to listen to their reasons for not telling me, I actually screamed for Ric and left. My blood pressure skyrocketed, and I knew I had to go, or I would say something I would regret later. Needless to say, I no longer hung out with that crowd. I need people I could trust around, especially now.

I haul into the marina and park in the sunny gravel lot across from the fish-gutting table next to a new Chevy pickup.

I grab my pocketbook and briefcase off the passenger's seat, stuff my cell phone into the briefcase with one hand while still holding half a Lemon pie ice cream cone in the other. I pop the trunk. I shove the cone in my mouth and grab the boat bag containing the keys, GPS, radio, sunblock, and other assorted necessities. I slammed the trunk with my forearm and headed over to walk down the dock. I note I might need two trips coming back to the car if I'm going to empty the boat safe.

I'm still laughing at the expression on Gert's face when I told her I had a safe with records of some of my personal stocks, investments, and some cash hidden beneath the couch on my boat. "There are records on that rigidly old thing!" Little did she know my boat is actually the safest place. I mean really, who would think to look on someone's boat for important paperwork. In a safe deposit box, maybe. On a boat, I think not.

Sunny days cleared my head. I should be grateful the weather gods gave me sunshine to deal with the clouds of my life. The clouds of my life were starting to part.

The weight of my baggage forced my shoulders to relax. I exhale the reality Sludge Puppy is going to be a victim of Jon and my break-up. I might just repurchase her after everything is settled. I forgot what we had decided that morning. Were we splitting the actual value of the boat or the cost to replace it? Gert definitely needed to go for today's value, so I could pick it up cheap.

Lost in my own world of sunshine, salt air, and a pending court battle, I didn't hear Molly until she caught up with me halfway down the dock.

"Hey, Maxi, did you forget to call and let me know you had someone coming by to work on your boat?" That's Molly—no small talk. At least she wasn't criticizing my driving or docking abilities.

The ice cream cone slipped from my mouth, fell on to the dock, tumbled into the water, creating a yellow ring. I mourned the loss. "What? I don't have anyone working on my boat." The remains of Lemon pie ice cream trailed down my skirt with a small pile melting on the dock. I brushed it into the water with my foot while I squinted down the pier and caught a glimpse of a tall man in a dark t-shirt standing near my space. "Who said that?"

"Well,, you got two guys and a woman down there now. Don't know what they are doing, but I can tell you they've been inside your cabin. Must have got the keys from somewhere."

"Oh, crap." I start to move away. Molly grabs my arm.

"I'll call the police. We should wait."

"Horse droppings. This had pond sucking scumbag written all over it. Molly, I know Jon has something to do with this, my gut says so." So much for me taking a break. "I'm going down there and yes, please, call the police. I'll need this on the record."

I trudge down the dock making as much noise as possible to announce my arrival. My top canvases were spread out over the main pier with my fishing gear piled up on the fingers. The cabin door lay wide open. Two men are having a heated discussion. Their faces scowled at each other. One had his hands deep in his pockets, while the other pointed at something in the cuddy. I didn't see the third person. I must admit walking down the dock to my boat alone while three complete strangers ransacked is probably not the brightest thing I'd ever done. Maybe Gert is right, I'm way too emotional.

"Nice boat," I called from the main dock as I made an effort to maneuver around my canvases. My hands were sticky from the ice cream. I held on to all my stuff, probably looking like the tourist from hell.

I caught them by surprise, even with my big entrance. One jumped, and the other dude's shoulders went up and then dropped back into position as he slowly turned to face me. He looked about forty-something, definitely had the tough guy vibe going. He got a lot bigger than he looked from the other end of the dock. He attempted a smile while giving me the up and down pore over before he spoke. I hated it when guys did that. His face went soft, yet his body tensed.

"Yep, she's a beauty," he gushed. He leaned back on his heels. In one move, he blocked my view into the cabin. He had on a dirty t-shirt and faded blue jeans. He tried to look casual, yet something about him oozed tension. Maybe it's the way he rocked on his heels or the fact his hands stayed in his pockets. Either way, there is no warmth or fuzzies. Worse, his accomplice had disappeared.

"That she is. Beautiful day to be on the water," My lame attempt to keep a conversation going while I glanced down the dock to see if the police had arrived. My muscles were cramping up from holding on to all my stuff. I wanted to knock this guy's lights out just for spite.

"Yes, it is," he replied, still doing the rocking thing.

"So, did you all catch anything? I heard blues are running." The bluefish wouldn't be running for another month or so, and from what I'd heard from a local fisherman, it didn't look like it's going to be that great of a season. Any self-respecting fisherman would know this, or at least it's not the season to catch this type of fish.

"Naw, we're just, you know, hanging out." I prayed silently; they didn't make guns so small they would fit into a jean pocket.

At this point, I had enough. I mean, this is still my property. My son had named the boat Sludge Puppy, after our lazy Labrador. The boat my husband had insisted I upgrade to buying new because a used boat just wouldn't do. My last sanctuary on earth, and this guy and his buds invaded my space, defacing it, taking away yet another piece of my sanity.

"It's mine." The guy didn't move. He just kept watching me with a tight smile on his face.

"This boat is yours?" he repeated on the loud side, nodding his head in the direction of the cabin.

"Yeah. Can I ask what you're doing on it?" I drop everything on the dock except my purse and fold my arms tight across my chest. I put a scowl on my face. I could hear sirens in the distance, and silently I cross my fingers. They are heading my way.

"This boat belongs to Jon Jacobs. Says so on my work order." He pulled out a crumpled piece of paper from his pocket and handed it to me. I straighten it out, and sure enough, it listed Jon as the vessel owner. The entire document is smudged except for Jon's name and the boat location. The hairs on the back of my neck rise. I get a sick feeling in my stomach. I know it wasn't from eating the lemon pie ice cream too fast.

"There has been a mistake. I am the vessel owner. And what did you say you were doing on my boat?" A woman, who looked to be about my age, emerged from below carrying a large briefcase. She's followed by the guy who I saw on deck earlier. She met the eye of the guy doing the talking, then strolled past me toward the parking lot—the other guy right behind her.

"Hey!" I yelled, but neither turned around. "What the heck?"

The talker stepped off the deck onto the dock. "I'll need to call my office," he starts to walk away. Without thinking, I grabbed his arm. He immediately reversed the hold, digging his hand into my upper arm and making fingerprints in my bicep. "Problem?" My arm throbs. His eyes went dark, and all I could think of is how stupid I am to not listen to Molly.

"No problem," My semi-tough girl voice doesn't seem so tough. He released me, turned, and walked away. I stood and stared, rubbing my arms where he had touched me. I peeked back at my boat and inhaled as much air as physically possible, feeling tentative about going inside. I had been violated, and I knew it had to be Jon who did this. He not only had to have the money, but he also had to make it wickedly uncomfortable for me to be anywhere. If he couldn't have the whole thing, he didn't want me to have any of it.

The boat is practically the symbol of our divorce. The Sludge Puppy went from being something of a complete joy to a bone of contention with each passing day. Jon wanted everything, except me.

"All I wanted to do is go out on my boat for the afternoon. Is that too much to ask?" I called up in the sky. "All I want is a little peace and…ewe!" A seagull shit on my shoulder. The glob of crap dripped down the front of my shirt. I sat down on the dock and cried. Not little girlie tears. Big two-year-old tantrum sobbing came out of me.

Not just for the boat, or the divorce, or the pressure of running the business, or not hearing from Zack, or seagull shit on my favorite purple suit, it is everything all at once! And I didn't like it. So, I cry, knowing I had to sell the damn boat to avoid contamination of sleazy people germs. I cried some more for ending up with a lower than pond scum sucking leach on society's butt I met at a Dead concert for a husband because I was desperate, lonely, and pregnant. I convinced myself he was my soul mate! I should know better than to marry a tour rat.

I sob because I still had to go to the supermarket and get food for supper. After all, Ric is going to be at Jon's house all weekend, I'm alone, and scared. Then I bawled some more because I could, and I didn't need a reason.

Within minutes of the "contractors" leaving, the Westbrook police showed up and searched the inside the boat for clues. I paced between the shiny new boat next to me and my craft, peeking into the cabin, yet not venturing on board, convinced Jon had sent those guys to plant a bomb and blow me to bits.

"Can you think of a reason your husband would hire a contractor?"

"My ex-husband, officer, and I don't know why. I just…" My voice cracked, and the tears started up again.

Ignoring my emotional state, he continued, "We couldn't find anything wrong, Mrs. Jacobs. I'm sorry. The cushions are scattered on the floor, but nothing seems missing. They were driving what looked like a new Chevy 4x4. We will check out the company name and truck license and get back to you." I shook his hand and thanked him. The police were here for less than fifteen minutes. I began to put the canvases on to lock up.

While I spoke with Officer Smiley, Molly had replaced the front cover and now lifted the back canvas in place. I peeked downstairs at the mess. The cushions of the couch were more than just removed. One had a significant slash in it. The whole couch looked funny like it had been placed off-balance somehow. Nothing made sense. My microwave sat shiny and new on the counter untouched—the television visible above the dining table. Nothing in the cabin looked or felt right.

I shut the cabin doors and turned my key while staring at the lock. There were scrapes on the top. I figure they must not mean anything if the police didn't comment. Together, we threw the fishing gear on top of the deck. Molly and I got everything back into place. Then, in silence, we walked down the dock back to the parking lot.

"Thanks, Molly," I said while trying to find my keys. "By the way, has Jon been here lately?" Molly knew about our battles, and I always got the impression she would give her right arm to stay neutral. Even asking is pushing the boundary.

"Once or twice with—" she stopped talking, and I didn't need to ask with whom. "Oh, and your lawyer gal was out here too. Just before those guys arrived. Said she was looking for you." Molly waited for my reaction. The only conclusion I could come to is Gert had something important to tell me in person. Without a doubt, the boat's gone. No way am I keeping it. Ric and I could pick out a new one after everything settled down. We could name it Sludge Puppy II or give it an entirely new name. I didn't care. I just needed to get rid of this one. My head hurt.

"Thanks again, Mol," I looked back down the dock, adding, "I think I'm going to sell her."

"That would probably be best." Molly is already walking away towards the clubhouse. I walked over to my car, looked back at the dock, get in, lock the door, and drive away.

Chapter Ten

I drove down Route one in Rhode Island, heading to Newport, though I could think of a hundred things I should be doing in Mayberry. Lunch with Bob Carlson had taken up most of my Monday. Then Jon and his boat inspectors ruined my Tuesday. Unbelievably, Jon is such a coward he still would not admit to sending those dirtbags to vandalize my boat. After I screamed at him for five minutes, he just called me crazy and hung up. His last words were, "Talk to my lawyer from now on."

I drove an hour and a half for a series of meetings.

Downtown Newport had that old shipping village feel to it. The cobblestone roads with quaint, expensive shops I am sure a hundred years ago sold provisions people actually needed instead of designer jewelry, clothing, and antiques. Of course, a hundred years ago, Newport was the playground for the glitzy rich and famous so not so much has changed

Attorney Mary Swintek's office is up on a hill just off the main drag. The place is definitely historical. She even had some plaque by the door, stating it was the home of Captain Richard Cook, one of the first settlers in Newport. The house had a creepy haunted feeling, yet when Mary walked out to meet me and shook my hand, all the creepiness vanished.

I liked Mary immediately. She talked a mile and minute, yet not wasting time.

"So, Maxi, how can I help?" She led me to a conference room that is much like a parlor from yesteryear. A beautiful lounge faced a bay window that looked upon the harbor. I would never get any work done here because I'd be watching the boats all day.

Mary's assistant, Marge, had placed a tray of iced tea and Italian cookies on the coffee table then vanished.

"Did Nancy explain our situation?" I sipped my tea, still in awe of my surroundings. Mary is the anti-Gert. She had on a soft flowing skirt with a solid top and Birkenstocks.

"She did a little," Mary answered while reaching behind her. She placed a folder with my name on it on the sofa. "From what I read, I may have a few suggestions," I nodded for her to continue, "the least painful for you would be to go franchise and sell the Newport publication to the rep that left. You've got to know this is a small town. It's important for all to save face, and politically, you don't want to be burning bridges."

"How would that work for her? I mean, why would she agree to this? The woman just quit on me, then the next thing I know, I'm getting calls from confused advertisers about this new publication."

"This is win-win, Max. Think about it. She gets a known quantity to sell, the publisher title she desperately seeks, and, here's the best part, you would still get residuals."

98

Wow, this woman is good! "I need to be honest, Mary, I'm thinking about selling the business. There is an offer on the table now. How would that affect both deals?"

"Well, if you sell the franchise to the Newport rep right away, you just make it part of the pending sale that she is a franchisee. You also allow Ms. Newport to opt-out of her franchise agreement with the new owners, but she would lose the publication."

"I'm liking the sound of all this." I helped myself to a victory cookie just as Jon popped into my mind. "Ah, Mary, there's one more thing." She waited for me to continue, "I'm in the process of getting divorced, so any money I get from a franchise sale would be split with my not soon enough ex-husband."

"Oh, Maxi, this is so easy. We'll distribute some of the proceeds in an account for your son, like a Roth IRA, and then give the rest as bonuses to your staff so your soon-to-be ex-husband won't be able to touch it."

I am in awe. "You are brilliant!" I wondered why Gert hadn't come up with a similar solution to the issue about the boat and other stuff I had to sell.

"I believe having a franchise set up for your out-of-state properties will also make your company more valuable to your buyer. It becomes turnkey for them in markets they aren't already in." Nancy's right again—Mary is terrific.

"How do we move forward?" I gave Mary Ms. Newport's phone number. That afternoon Mary and I met with the old rep, came up with a price that sounded reasonable, and agreed to move forward with the franchise sale immediately. We also discussed my pending decision with Bob Carlson. Mary, Ms.

Newport, and I decided to put in the sale agreement the parent company would assist with printing and other hard costs in exchange for no more than ten percent of the gross profits. And, if the parent company was ever sold, the franchisee would take on the full responsibility of the guide in their area and would have the option to renegotiate any deals with the new owners or spin-off on their own. This provision did not include publications in the parent company's home state.

I knew Bob. He would take the ten percent and look to negotiate more revenue by taking on production and distribution. This is still a respectable deal for Ms. Newport, as she would become, in addition to having the publisher title, a highly compensated salesperson as long as she didn't get lazy. But her laziness is no longer my problem.

I also got her to agree to take ownership immediately and take the responsibility of distributing the guides she forgot in her storage unit.

After these legal matters were settled, I called the two folks I was there to interview and canceled, saying they might want to give the new owner a call.

I am floating when Mary and I left the Ocean Coffee Roasters. "Please send your bill to Nancy," I instruct.

"Will do, and please keep me in mind for more projects," she adds. "I am licensed in Connecticut too."

I got in my car and called Nancy to give her the overview. "Nancy, this lady is amazing. Here it is three in the afternoon, and Newport is settled."

"I knew she would be," Nancy replied.

Thursday morning, I sit in my office to wait to hear from someone with good news because my horoscope said I would get some fantastic news this morning. Actually, it read, "This morning will bring you uplifting news that will carry you through the rest of the week. Be ready to notice it, or you will miss this opportunity." Well, I am ready and waiting!

I am raring to go. Ric is ready downstairs and waiting for me. We are running early. Of course, then it happened. The karma gods decided to play an evil joke on me.

At the beautiful age of forty-something, I have the luxury of zits and wrinkles, yes I am doubly blessed. I buy this unique all-natural zit stuff from the local health food store. It worked well with my skin. The lotion came in a glass tube with a roller on top, allowing the user to blast the zit directly, unlike the creams that dried out the surrounding areas.

I had just finished drying my hair, applying my moisturizer, and getting half-dressed when I reached for the tube. I removed the cap. It slipped from my fingers, bounced off the pedestal sink, took a swift shot off the back of the toilet, and landed in the toilet.

I watched this happen in what looked like slow motion. As I looked down into the toilet, I knew my first thought of leaving a note for the man of the house to get it out would be useless. The only man of the house is ten, watching cartoons downstairs, and no matter how much I offered, Ric would not stick his hand in the crapper.

I had two choices. I could call a plumber, pay an obnoxious amount of money to remove it, and become the subject of another pathetic female joke, or I could stick my hand in there and be done with it. I chose the latter.

In case you were wondering, toilet water is freezing even in the middle of the summer. The damn thing couldn't be more lodged in if I had planted it. After removing my shirt, I plunged my arm in. The stupid cap wouldn't budge. I tried flushing, thinking the water in motion would dislodge it. No, luck there. I slipped my bathrobe back on and headed downstairs to the junk drawer.

I rifled through rubber bands, masking tape, and screws, finally grabbing a wrench that looked like it might fit. Holding it in my right hand, I walked passed my child, mesmerized by Scooby-Doo.

The damn wrench wouldn't fit. I threw it in the sink and went in search of needle-nose pliers. How did I know what needle-nose pliers looked like? My dad taught me Well,. He also made sure my junk drawer contained all the essential tools. I had a wrench, needle nose pliers, regular pliers, a hammer, and duct tape. There is also spare change, extra keys, plenty of pens and pencils, and parts. Parts of what I had no clue. All I knew is the day I threw one out I'd be in the hardware store paying up the nose for it because it would suddenly go somewhere.

Back to the toilet, I went. I put my hand and the pliers into the frigid water and leveraged my arm against the side, ready to pull out the culprit. I held tight and could feel it giving. After pinning my arms around the rim of the toilet, I can wedge the cap free. With a victory punch in the air, I dropped it into the wastebasket and tossed the pliers and wrench in the sink. I took the bar of soap, turned on the hot water, and scrubbed my hands clean. I stared at the tools.

"Can't put them back in the junk draw," I said out loud. I reached into the cabinet and pulled out the bottle of bleach I used for cleaning. I poured the bleach on top and left the contaminated tools in the sink. I would explain later if someone asked.

I got dressed again and rushed Ric out the door.

"I was ready on time, Mom. Today this is your fault," Ric grumbled all the way to camp.

It is always my fault. After the morning's excitement, my heartbeat had finally slowed from the stress of running late. After dropping Ric off and making it to work without incident, I sat in my office to evaluate our situation.

Nancy was the charmer earlier too. "So, did you hit the gym this morning?" she inquired when I arrived, then proceeded to walk away laughing. I wanted to tell her to kiss off, but in the past whenever I swore she'd just laugh harder. I let the comment go and sulked in my office.

I want my parents to take Ric for a little vacation, but the separation agreement requires permission from Jon. I would need to explain to both parties why. How could I make my parents understand my sense of security had been taken away by some unknown force that insisted on inhibiting my space? On the flip side, how could I ask Jon for permission without accusing him of starting my insecurities?

My parents will think I am overreacting, their usual response to anything out of the ordinary happening in my life.

"Are you just overreacting again, Max? I'm sure it's not that bad."

I shudder. Actually, I owed my mother a call. She had left two messages. I should let her know about the latest events in my life, but then again, why worry her?

Bob left another reminder about Friday. I think he is losing his edge. I waited on Gert. Maybe this would finish the whole divorce thing, and I could move on. I could launch another publication, "The Unfabulous Dining Guide," to include a list of places you shouldn't eat on a dare. I could recommend what not to eat and give disgusting descriptions of the food, so people would understand why they should avoid it. The better restaurants could buy ads that read, "Eat Here! We're not featured!"

My hand hit my head. I had been hanging around little boys too much. Next thing you knew, I will be the promoter for the National Burping Contest or, better yet, Fart-Aholics Anonymous.

Then again, maybe I should take the money and move with Ric to a smaller place in town where we could start over. We'd stay in Mayberry until Ric left for college, then downsize to a neighborhood Jon could never afford. I'd never see him walking the dog or sitting his butt on my beach or just being in my sight zone. That would be nice.

The most significant contributor to my nasty state of mind is Zack, who still has not called. Also, my brother Pete hadn't called me back either. I am on the brink of another twenty-year mystery. I can understand Zack not calling—Well, not really—but I felt lenient towards him since it had taken him years to follow up on the last phone call. Pete rated lower than dog crap in my book for not returning my 911 call. I cut my brother no slack. Besides, I had convinced myself that if I talked to Pete, he could fill in the missing link on Zack. Also, Pete couldn't stand Jon from the day they met, so I am hoping he could come up with some ways to move things along and fix my mess of a life. With his MBA and a law degree, Pete is exceptional at coming up with ways to get people to do what he wanted, especially when it came to money matters. And he did it all within the law.

It's not that I didn't trust Gert, I trusted her with my life, but sometimes it seemed more important to her to be tough and win a battle than to fully fix a situation. I couldn't help but think about Newport and how quickly that situation was taken care of on the heels of Mary's advice. Meanwhile, months had passed. My divorce drags on. Every time we got back into negotiations, I wound up losing more! In the beginning, Jon hadn't wanted anything except his freedom. Then he wanted his stuff. After that, half the house. Now it's the boat, my business, plus stocks and such. I didn't understand how he went from nothing to wanting it all. We had settled this in the first week. Then he had met Luke at the Monkey Bar, the sleaziest joint in town, and the next thing I know, months later, the negotiations move from bad to worse.

Gert said she was taking care of it, but if she said "compromise" one more time I am going to scream. Maybe I should listen to Nancy and get a second opinion. Then again, why rock the boat? It wouldn't be mine much longer anyway.

There are stacks of paperwork surrounding me that need my total attention, and I couldn't concentrate on anyone.

Nancy fielded all calls and avoided putting anyone through who might aggravate me. How she could tell the difference between this and PMS, God only knows. I think she may feel guilty for busting my butt earlier. Kicking anyone when they were already down is no fun.

I lean back in my chair, close my eyes, and hope for divine intervention or at least some form of clarity.

Nothing. Maybe I need food. Food would be good, like crab cakes or more of beet soup. Wow, that was terrific soup, especially when it was on Zack's breath. I slap the side of my head a little too hard this time. If I kept hitting myself, I'll give yours truly a concussion soon. Maybe I need to hear the voice of a member of the opposite sex who genuinely cares about my Well,-being. Hmmm, I could call my dad. Then again, maybe I didn't need to hear his voice either.

Grabbing my purse, I tell Nancy on where I am heading and when I'll be back. She took off her glasses and pointed at me.

"Don't forget Max, you have a conference call at three so don't get too lost." Nancy sounded precisely like a teacher scolding a kindergartener for peeing in the corner when the kid was just told she's not allowed to use the bathroom.

I drive to the point and grab a chocolate chip mint ice cream cone from one of the cart vendors. It's not beet soup, but who really needs beet soup on a ninety-degree day. I decide I like this place. It had calm, and peacefulness, the way my life had been before Jon

106

came into it. Maybe I'd move into one of those condos that overlooked the place. I looked around and noticed the point can be as lonely too.

I took a seat on one of the many scattered benches away from the day-trippers to watch the river traffic, barges, sailboats, and fishing vessels pass by, all heading out to Long Island Sound. I wish I was on one of those boats instead of sitting here in my suit. Just the act of sitting here had my shoulders creeping back down to where they are supposed to be. Maybe this is all I need. I inhale deeply and exhale on a ten count. My back cracked in the process. I watch the waves float in and out, the seagulls swarm around the picnickers. Yeah, I'm in freakin' paradise.

I finish off the cone and pull my cell phone out of my pocket. Pressing menu, I hit Pete's super-secret number, the one Uncle Sam assigned, and all the family members were instructed to use for emergencies only. My life falling apart constitutes an emergency, and my brother better answer his damn phone, or I'd track him down wherever he is in the world, being more crazed than the communist dictator he was sabotaging or, worse yet, more psychotic than his wife PMSing. (She once got so angry with my brother she switched tables in a restaurant to eat with what looked like a more delightful family than hers. She just left him and the kids sitting there with their mouths hanging open while she smiled and dined with strangers. She even convinced the other people to pick up the bill for her meal.)

One ring, two rings, three rings, voice mail. Figured. I wait for the beep. "Listen, you slime sucking piece of dirt, I don't care if you are out saving the world. My life is falling apart, and I need my brother right now, so call me!" I yell into a piece of plastic that may or may not be actually connected to another part of plastic owned by my brother. "And next time you give my number to an old friend, warn me first! This isn't going to be like the call to the condo. I want details! Oh, and I love you and be careful." I pound the end button, closed my eyes, sat back, and tried to slow my breath and slow my heartbeat.

When I open my eyes, a little old lady peered at me, with her face scrunched up like she is trying to focus.

"I don't mean to pry…

Yeah right. Prying is second nature to gossip when you live in a small town.

"…but you look like you need help. Do you need help?"

I actually had to think about that. Did I need help? I am about to answer when a gray-haired gentleman in plaid slacks and a "Worlds Sexiest Grandpa" t-shirt walked over.

"Ethel," he bellowed, "bug out. She could be crazy. Having a breakdown. She'll probably throw ya in the drink."

Did I look that bad?

"Edmund, please don't upset her more." She reached into her purse and handed me a lifesaver. "She needs a mother. Do you have a mother, dearie?"

"I do," I say. "She's even crazier than me."

The lady hurried back by her husband. Edmund winked at me as I add, "Thank you for the lifesaver."

Could my day get any stranger? Maybe I should call my mother and let her and Dad know what Jon had

108

been up to. Plus, I bet Mom could get Pete to call back. She's a real pro at the whole guilt trip thing. She had learned from the best, her mother, also known as my grandmother. My grandma could get you to drive across town in a snow storm to bring her ice cream because she thought ice cream would be a nice dessert after dinner, and she didn't have any in the freezer.

After you took your life in your hands spinning your car out on icy roads to get there, she would tell you that you brought the wrong brand or flavor, but it was OK, it would do. Then came the sigh. I always hated the sigh because I knew after the sigh, I would go back out into the storm to get the right kind, even though she insisted what I had bought would do. God, I love my grandma.

Everything with my family had always come topped with a bit of guilt for good measure. Whoever said no good deed goes unpunished must be a descendent on my mother's side, or on my father's side, for that matter. Maybe it is an Italian thing.

I punch in shift M and hit send. Seconds later, my mother's voice resonated in my phone, another answering machine. I always pictured them puttering around the house all day. I couldn't believe they actually went out!

"Hi, Mom, it's Max. I just wanted to let you and Dad know everything's okay. Someone tried to break into the boat, so after very little rational thought, I am putting her up for sale. It is contaminated with sleaze germs. I don't feel comfortable with it anymore. Oh, and Dad, I will ask for more than I paid as you taught me. I'm wondering if you might want Ric for a couple days next week? Nothing pressing, I thought you could have some grandparent quality time. Let me know. Your soon-to-be-ex son-in-law is dragging us back into court on Monday. What a life! If you hear from Pete…" BEEP. Cut off at the pass. I thought the part about my boat getting broken into would prompt a callback. I could ask about Pete then if I could get a word into the conversation.

The sunshine reflected on the water, playing tricks on my eyes. On the back of a hundred-thousand-dollar cigarette boat, I swear I see Gert and Hillsey bouncing along. I rub my eyes. No – it couldn't be. There is way too much on my mind.

I sulk back into my office intent on checking emails and other essential things. All my deadlines passed, advertisers billed, guides printed, and the only worry, distribution, which isn't a worry because Nancy's in charge of that. She couldn't stand to see the boxes pile up in what is supposed to be our lobby, so she makes sure every single one gets to where it is supposed to be. We usually hire a temp in the summer. She said something about someone applying. I should pay more attention because if she didn't hire someone, then I guess I would add delivery person to my title.

I had no real worries until August. Then it would be time to sell the fall book, renew a few contracts, and hire replacements for those who jump ship. Let's not forget to get Ric ready for school, start back into whatever fall sport he'll do, and basically get his life in order. I guess I should feel grateful I had parts of my life I could count on to be routine. This is maybe even stable, stable being a relative term.

The business is another example of Murphy's Law in action since this is part of my life I am giving up. Go figure.

Chapter Eleven

I am playing solitaire on my computer. To the untrained eye, it looks like I am knee-deep in work, but I haven't done a darn thing since I got back. Nancy gave directions to the new delivery guys on how to get to the storage area and then went over there to set up for their first run. She still insists there is something fishy about the two of them.

"Maxi, it just doesn't feel right. They had a brand new truck, and they were delivering guides for minimum wage." Her red hair swayed back and forth while she shook her head. "I'm telling you, I have a bad feeling."

My hand raises to stop her before she voices another one of her conspiracy theories regarding my life. "Nance, do *you* want to do deliveries?"

"With all the work I have here already?"

I put my hand back up. "Then hire them. Pay them minimum wage. Let them figure out the gas costs more than they're making."

"Maxi, I just…." Nancy sat across from me at my desk. I'd seen that worried look before. "Maybe you should meet them too?"

"No, I don't have time."

My refusal brought out the pout. Man, that woman had perfected the bottom lip sad eyes pout face.

I actually started to feel guilty. Wow! I thought only my mother had the power.

"Nancy, I understand. Gut feeling and all. But we need a delivery person. I don't have time to make the deliveries, and neither do you, so we need to hire these people. Don't give them complete access; just the storage shed. They'll probably quit next week anyway." My last comment got her smiling.

"Ok, Max, I'll hire them." Nancy got up and walked out, shouting back, "But if they screw up, it's on you, not me."

Nancy's parting words popped into my head, and I laugh. Everything that happened lately was my fault. What did I care anyhow? I might not own the company by next week.

I went back to beating my high score on solitaire. I didn't have a speck of ambition. I made the decision to sell. I needed to say it aloud.

"I'm going to . . ." This is harder than I thought. "I'm going to…" Ok, one more time. "I'm going to call my dad and see what he thinks." I lean forward and hit the speaker, then punch in my parents' number.

"Hello." My dad answered on the first ring.

"Hey, Dad, it's Max. What's happening?" I lean back to hear my dad chuckle.

"What do you think is happening? Did they catch the people who were trespassing on your boat?"

"Not yet. Soon," I said, trying to convince both of us it will happen. "I got something I want to run by you…" I told him the whole Bob Carlson story and described the deal on the table. "What do you think?

"I don't know. I didn't know you were interested in selling."

"I didn't know either. I think it's the easiest way out. I could sell off the business, the boat, and some stock."

"Maxi, you don't sell a stock. You live off the interest. Didn't I teach you anything?"

"Dad, I could give Jon half, so he'll go away." Hearing those words aloud made me see how dumb the idea really is. He'd want more. He always did.

"What does your lawyer say?"

"She says it's a good deal, and I should do it."

"Figures, she would say that."

"Well,, what do you think?" I put my ear to the speaker, waiting for some words of wisdom to make my life better.

"I think you can do better."

That wasn't what I was expecting, so I asked the obvious, "How, Dad?"

"Well,, they came to you, right?"

I nodded yes, even though he couldn't see me.

"Maybe there is more that could be brought to the table. I'd try to find a way to hide some of the proceeds from your ex."

Boy, he said that as if he's spitting on Jon.

"Maybe look into a trust fund for Ric or something. That way, he can't touch any of the money."

"So, do you think I should sell?" I chewed on my lower lip.

"Maxi, I think you should do whatever will make you happy. If it were me, I'd sell it. That fancy lawyer of yours can draw up an agreement that says with acceptance of this payment you are done with Jon. But that's me."

"Great idea, Dad." I shook my head and beamed. "Thanks." Now, why didn't Gert come up with that?

"Anytime. Do you want to speak to your mother?"

My extrasensory perception told me she stood right next to him.

"I'd love to, but I need to go back to work."

He started laughing again. "I'll tell her you said hello."

"Thanks, Dad. Oh, and could you guys think about taking Ric for a few days next week? I have a lot to work out down here."

"Send him up," my mother shouted in the background.

"You hear that?"

"Yeah. Thanks. Love you guys." I hung up the phone and loosened up in my chair. I did have work to do, and I didn't want to do it.

My dad is right. Jon would come back for more. I have to figure out how to stop him.

I got up and paced. I grabbed my keys and purse, headed out of my inner office. Nancy was nowhere to be seen, probably still showing the delivery guys around. I wrote a quick note to her.

I talked to Dad. It all makes sense. I'm going to call Bob and say yes, under the condition you can come too. We are almost retired! I went to get Ric so we can hang out before he goes to scumbags. Have a great weekend!

I left the note on her chair, so she'd see it when she got back. Then I took off for the day. I skipped over to my car and saw my reflection in the window. Did I actually look happy? "Life is getting better."

Chapter Twelve

At two o'clock in the morning, I lay on the couch in my living room, staring into the darkness. I keep hearing scraping sounds on the side of the house, clicks, bumps, and swishes, followed by a clunk. I knew it couldn't be the heat because, in summer, the furnace is not on. I am sweating because I didn't run the air conditioner; that way, I could hear the scary noises clearly and use my imagination to figure out their source.

Ric is at his father and the Tart's house. I got him there exactly at five and informed Jon he needed to bring him back to my place at five on Sunday. Any later and I would call the police. I am still upset over the boat. Jon again denied knowing anything about the contractors. "Why would I do that, Max," he countered. "We agreed to sell it."

With that comment, I took it upon myself to be the biggest bitch in the world to him. At last, I had a tangible reason to give the prick what he deserved. Okay, so I'm a little irrational. My ex-boyfriend *had* named me psycho bitch long before Jon ever met me, because of the way I PMS'd during the time we had dated. In his case, the guy was absolutely correct, at that point in my life, I was a lunatic.

But what had I learned since then? When Jon messed with my life, I let him. When he tried to take my pride, I let him. When he went after my boat, he pissed me off, yet I let him. But when he tried to leverage and take away my son in the deal, he crossed the line. I wanted him to know whom he is up against in case he had any more fancy ideas of using our son to his advantage. This is not going to happen!

My life got even better when I arrived home. The message light on my answering machine flashed. Wouldn't you know it, I had missed Pete's call. I loved the message too. "Hey, Max, you're not there. OK, Well, I'll try back when I can. By the way, this is Pete." You think I wouldn't know my own brother's voice. I immediately dialed his line again and again got the machine. I didn't bother leaving a message — missed connections — the story of my life.

I had one of my complete evenings tonight. I started with Chinese to go. Vegetarian lo mien and fried veggie dumplings are done to perfection. I must look either like a nice person or a real loser because the owner threw in a couple cucumber rolls too. He offered me a new milk drink, but just the smell made me want to throw up. Politely, without wrinkling my nose in disgust, I declined his offer by saying I am lactose intolerant. He shook his head and giggled every time he walked past.

Here's the problem with the current state of my life. People couldn't even be friendly to me without me suspecting something. It's too bad I am training myself to think this way. Maybe this is something I should change about myself. I'll add it to the list.

My night got even better when I got lucky with an Elvis movie marathon on TBS. I got to watch Elvis with Shelly Fabres while they strutted on the beach, drove race cars, and babysat a gangster's daughter. I dozed off when the movie set in Hawaii started up. You know the one where Elvis turned down, running a multi-million-dollar pineapple business to become a travel agent. Not *Blue Hawaii*, the other one. Or maybe this is *Blue Hawaii*, I'm not sure.

Boy did Elvis and I have the life. I mean, what else could a person need? Good music, good parties, and good lovin'. Alright, so that didn't exactly describe my current life, and this is all make-believe, and the movie took place before I was born, but this is Elvis, and I am sitting on the couch pretending it's me too. He was the king!

I woke up for the second time. The first time I dozed with the television on. When my twenty-four-hour cable channel decided to test the emergency broadcast system at midnight, that annoying tone woke me up. Elvis is still shaking and singing, so it is easy to fall back asleep. With a touch of the remote, the house plunged back into silence. I am dreaming about surfing in paradise with Elvis, which is an excellent trick since he'd been dead for over twenty years, and I do not know how to surf. In my dream, he's movie-Elvis, as opposed to last-days-Elvis. The Elvis with the great body and soulful eyes as opposed to the too many fried peanut butter and banana sandwich Elvis. Dawn of the old, fat, and wrinkled, a look into my future.

When I awoke, my stomach did flips. My heart beat faster than I think it should, and as much as I tried

118

taking deep yoga breaths, nothing slowed down. Something's not right.

During these crazy nights when my mind ran wild, I wished Jon hadn't taken the dog, or better yet, I wish I had gone out and got another one at the pound. I needed a big ex-police dog now, one that would growl at the real noises, sleep through the fake ones, and attack on command. Like my Labrador did, only more robust and more intimidating. I had a dog like that when I lived with my parents. I would wake up at night shaking with a cold sweat, no clue why. But then I'd look at Candy lying on the floor by my bed and figure if she wasn't moving, everything is okay.

I didn't get another dog because Gert had suggested when Ric visited his father, I should take off somewhere for an adventure instead of being home in the dark by myself. It sounded like a great idea. I actually believed I would do.

I wanted to sell the house, but Gert advised me to wait until after the divorce. She warned if I moved beforehand, Jon would be entitled to half the proceeds plus part of my new space when I decided to sell. So, I stayed even though I found a place I liked in another part of town. I decided when my divorce is final, the first thing Ric and I would do would be to move to a secure, gated condo complex with a pool and docking privileges, so I could actually dock a new boat outside my condo. Wouldn't that be cool?

"Just stop this," I whisper into the silence.

I am not calming down, and my imagination is taking off in all directions. In my mind, the scraping sound in the kitchen became someone trying to break in through the windows. No one would notice them there because of the enormous rhododendron bush blocking the view from the street. I could hear the scratch scratch of a knife making its way into the locks.

My wind chimes had been ringing throughout the night. Yet, the air outside is abnormally still, at least as far as I could tell from looking at the branches of the big pine tree out the picture window. Usually, the chimes rang when the porch door opened, but I hadn't heard the hinges squeak. Maybe that didn't mean anything since I am concentrating so hard on the scraping at the window.

Both the downstairs and upstairs basement doors were locked, I had made sure of that before it got dark out. I had also checked the upstairs closets. Once back downstairs, I knew I wouldn't venture back up until daylight. Ok, I admit it. I am a little flaky when it came to unidentifiable noises and being alone in the house at night. I guess it stemmed from when I was a kid, and the folds of my blankets were snakes moving towards me, or the clicking of the radiator was some horrible beast beside my bed. I've been known to be a little paranoid in the dark and overconfident in the light.

I had locked my office and spare room. I told myself to ignore any noises from either, since once inside, the intruder would need to break down a door. I could run out the front of the house, where I had strategically parked my car at the end of the driveway for a fast escape. My cell phone and pocketbook were already under a sweatshirt on the front seat.

The only rooms left for me to obsess about now were the living room, kitchen, and bathroom, all essential to my existence. I thought about checking into a hotel. What a waste of money that would be! It would kill me to pay in-season rates. I most likely wouldn't be able to get a room anyhow. On Saturday nights during high season, few places had vacancies. In all probability, I wouldn't sleep any better in a hotel. I need to face the fact on my weekends alone, I'll be staying up all night.

Speaking of staying up all night, I wonder what Zack is doing right now? God, how I wish he had never called! The spell had been recast, like a flashback to junior high. How could someone get another person so worked up? I stretched my body back out and shivered while my muscles untightened a little. I moved a violet cotton blanket to cover all of me. I reached over to the coffee table and took a sip from the lukewarm glass of water I had left there earlier.

Come on, Max, it was one date. Don't get overexcited now. Don't go back there. It's not worth it to fill your mind with Zack Brady. You have other things to concentrate on. Remember, been there done that once, oh no wait. Been there, done that twice. What do they say, three times a charm? Or is it three strikes and you're out?

I am determined to stop thinking about negatives. After all, he's on guy time, so maybe I would hear from him in a week or so. Or possibly, like last time, it would be a few years. I closed my eyes and tried to picture Zack sitting across the table from me. I couldn't see his face, too much shadow, but I could make out the outline of his hair and jaw.

I took in a deep breath and exhaled. I stretched my arms above my head, reached my feet past the end of the couch, and some of the strain slipped away. I repositioned the blanket again, taking the time to tuck it under my toes.

I am going to be ok. I could handle all this. My life isn't all that bad. Better than most actually. I closed my eyes and returned to the beach with Elvis.

Chapter Thirteen

I am lost in dreamland. The place appeared familiar. I'm in a dark room with a spinning mirrored ball that reflected little drops of rainbow-colored light across the walls and ceiling. The movement of the swirling colors made me dizzy. There were pillows and shadows of people around the perimeter, and I caught a whiff of my grandmother's spare room—a musty, old car smell.

Music is coming from another area, and I followed the sound. Who is this? Earth, Wind, and Fire! This couldn't be anywhere I would actually be seen. Pop music, yuk! People stood around, talking in groups. The girls laughed aloud. Everyone is skinny in suede vests over halter tops with Jordache jeans? And paisley tops. This is getting strange.

I whacked my forehead.

This is the room in the Community Center in the town I grew up. A former elementary school had been converted into a gym, billiards room, disco dance room, and space where meetings and adult classes were held.

I made an attempt to remember my way as I squeezed past people in the hallway, still following the sound. No one noticed me, like in high school, as I crept closer to the entrance. White lights are flashing, colored lights spinning, loud distorted music, and now…it sounded like Boston. More than a feeling. I am definitely in the seventies!

I clapped my hands over my head as I pushed through the door. The crowd momentum carried me to the other side. Some of the faces appeared familiar though I couldn't remember names.

It is uncomfortably hot. I am nauseous like I had drunk too much Reunite wine on an empty stomach. The room spun with more flashing lights. My body swung back against the outer rim. Still, instead of hitting the wall, I hit a person who immediately put his arms around my waist.

I struggled to see who is holding me. A voice whispered in my ear, "It's ok, Max. I got you now. I will take care of you, I promise. Don't be afraid."

I relaxed a little, feeling his warm body against mine, his warm breath swirling around my ear. Everyplace we touched tingled with tiny jolts of electricity. I noticed the blue swirly stars shooting across the ceiling.

Together we moved slowly to the music, rubbing our bodies against each other, even though the rhythm of the song and the other people in the room jumped around much faster. Quivers of heat moved in the right spots of my body.

"Max, I'm on your side. Trust me. It will be alright, I promise."

I forced my head back around to see Zack's brown eyes gazing back at me. That feeling of being under a warm comforter while watching TV on a cold winter day took over, and excitement pulsated through my body.

With a deep sigh, I opened my eyes, and Jon is in Zack's place. His arms are wrapped around my body, too tight, while he screeched in my ear.

"I got you now, Maxi. Who's going to save you now?" The shrieking became louder, painfully loud. Hillsey stood behind him with a group of the mean girls, pointing at me and sneering. The lights flickered faster, and the room spun. Zack is pushed up against the wall on the other side, fighting to get loose as the crowd held him back. I extended for him, but Jon detained me by the waist. I screamed without a sound coming from my throat. Please, Zack, rescue me!

BANG. I sat upright on the couch and examined the living room. I shivered from the cold and from being soaked with sweat. BANG! That noise. It is coming from my porch. Oh shit! I tried not to move. A beam of light circled around the kitchen and living room walls.

Someone is on my porch! CRASH! Things were falling. Whoever is there is moving stuff around. Searching, maybe, but for what? Oh crap! I'm sure I am about to have a heart attack. Or worse. Could I reach the phone? Maybe not. I could run out the front. And go where? My car. I thought I might be able to make it to my car. Shit. Shit! SHIT!

Someone is breaking into my house, and I am hyperventilating instead of thinking. I had never been in a room while someone broke into before, but I'm sure the normal human reaction is to lose it!

Because I am in the living room, I would know as soon as they get through. I surveyed around for an option. I could run upstairs and lock the door to my bedroom, but that door is so flimsy, even I could kick it down. I would be trapping myself.

But wait. I could go into Ric's room and climb out the window onto the roof of the porch, but that is the same porch where the intruder is attempting to break into my kitchen, so he would hear my pounce on the roof and come out and climb up the drainpipe and….

I examined the living room. The TV remote, an empty wine bottle, and a bowl of something were on the coffee table in front of me. There were empty Chinese food containers in a bag beside the table that reeked like leftover greasy food. There's a pile of magazines under the table. Ric had forgotten to put away his Lego's, which lay scattered under the end table. The cordless phone is on the floor. THE CORDLESS PHONE IS ON THE FLOOR!

Now the beam of light came through the windows and moved slowly across my kitchen. The door had a limited view of the room, yet whoever it is could still see too much into the house for my peace of mind.

I had to take my chances. Ducking down, I reached the cordless and dialed 911. I knew the light of the phone shined on the kitchen wall. I knew if I spoke, the intruder would most likely hear me because it is so quiet. I also knew the police would not instantly appear on my doorstep.

"911 Emergency. This is Sergeant Montgomery."

I communicated as soft as possible, "Someone is breaking into my house." My hand is over the headset as I viewed the light beam, still moving.

"I can't hear you, ma'am. Could you speak louder?"

Idiot, if I could talk louder, I would. "Someone is breaking into my house," I made an effort again with more urgency in my whisper. The scraping sounds were getting louder, and I now could hear two voices coming from my porch, both deep, probably male. "I need help."

"I can't hear you, ma'am. I'm going to send an officer over to your address. Please hold."

Holy crap! I'm on hold while two men were on my porch, rifling through my stuff and picking my back-door lock. While I half-listened to hold music and half-listened to the clink, clank, scrape at the door, I attempted to come up with another alternative. I could get to the front door, but it usually stuck, so it wouldn't open fast, especially in the high summer humidity.

Also, they might be the third guy out front, on the lookout. On lookout? I couldn't sit here anymore and wait. I slid off the couch and began crawling across the floor to the front door. Thankfully the loveseat blocked the view of the floor from the kitchen. Nobody ever sat in the loveseat, but I kept it as a laundry folding station. The loveseat is the only new looking piece of furniture in my place.

With any luck make I could make it into the hall by the front door. Every touch of the floor sounded like an elephant stumbling across the room. Weirdly, I am relieved to still hear the scraping sounds as I reach the front door. I lean in to listen. Nothing.

Reaching up, I turn the lock on the doorknob. CLICK. Shit. I didn't realize the lock would make so much noise. I froze. The rustle on the porch continued, and I swore I heard a car door out front. *Please send more than one cop*, I prayed silently.

A loud whistle sounded in the distance.

"Oh shit!" Doors slammed on the porch, and a sea of blue lights decorated the front of my house. I jerk open the front door and run headlong into Officer Miller of the town police department, startling both of us, except he had a distinct advantage of being the one holding the gun.

"Get back in the house, lock the damn door, and don't come out unless you hear from me," he shouted. I ran back inside, slammed the door shut, and threw my body against it, sliding to the floor in a big lump.

People screamed. Heavy footsteps ran by. I made out firecrackers exploding, although it could have been gunfire, and who knows what else is happening since I am stuck inside and can't see out. The only thing working is my imagination, which is quickly overloading and creating war movie scenes. Flashing blue emergency lights swirled across the walls in my living room and kitchen. Between the lights and shadows, overgrown figures appeared and disappeared. I put my hand on my chest and watched it move up and down with every heartbeat. My mouth filled with vomit. I have to use the bathroom, but I am too scared to move.

"I hate this. I hate this. I hate this," I rock back and forth, holding my knees close to my chest. "Why didn't you take that karate course, Max? No time, right? Bet you wish you had the time now." The voice in my head pestered. "Yeah, like karate could stop a bullet," I answered back. *"Party pooper,"* the little voice in my head retorted. I hated that voice in my head. My cynical

128

self only showed up at the most inopportune times. I wished I could banish it outside in the middle of the mayhem, far away from me. Maybe I could get it to take a bullet in the process. I had been told it was a Virgo thing. The theory that when Virgos fell under stress, they only looked at the terrible parts of the situation, never seeing what positive aspects exist.

I had spent years trying to train myself to see a glass half full. I thought I had it together. Maybe that little voice would get taken away with the loonies who were trying to break in. I shut my eyes and prayed for this all to be over. There is nothing rational left for me to do.

I inhale. One, two, three, four, five, I push my breath out. My body tightened to the point where I am cramping in the worst possible places. If I had to run, I didn't think I'd be able to. My hips crack. My thighs burn, and my upper back is so tight there is no way I could throw a punch.

There is a quiet knock on the front door.

"Max, open up."

The voice is familiar.

"Max, it's me, Zack."

I flung open the door, dove into his arms, and started sobbing uncontrollably.

"It's ok, Max. I'm here," he comforted.

My body shook all over. The stress flowed out of me with the touch of a familiar warm body. He embraced me tight, rubbing my back with one hand while wiping away my tears with the sleeve of the other.

"How did you….?" My voice trailed off. The only thing I feel is his hot body against mine, and his strong arms around me. Oh great, I am having another dream. Or I am in a trap and hallucinating. My body trembles as Zack tightens his grip. My breathing gradually slowed. My heart changed to a quiet beat inside my chest. The Mayberry police walked into my house and started to give a report, directing all the information to Zack.

"They got away, but there is a car parked in the middle of the road without plates about a block away. We are taking prints hoping to find something."

"I'd like a copy of anything you find out," Zack instructed. The officer nodded and disappeared through my kitchen. I pulled back, looked around, and observed the whole scene. Three cruisers were parked out front, and I could see some of my neighbors out on their front lawn. Two voices came from my back porch, and I figured at least two more officers are looking for clues.

I recognized another cop from the gym I try to attend. He wandered down my street with a huge dog, toward where they said the mystery car is parked. I vowed to get me one of those — a dog, not the cop — although the way my life had been going, I should consider both.

Zack moved me over to the couch, where I sat and stared at nothing. He is talking into his cell phone. I started watching his jaw tense then release. His hand made the same motion, tightening his fingers into a fist, then stretching them out. He hadn't shaven and had the rock star sexy five o'clock shadow. God, he's gorgeous! I couldn't make out what he is saying since his body is angled away from me. But I kept pinching myself to verify the scenario is real.

Zack repositioned himself, facing towards me and scooted closer. He reached over to take both my hands in his. "Max," he said in a tired voice, "a lot is going on here I can't explain right now. I can tell you, you can't stay here. I'm sorry, but you need a safer place to be."

"Duh," is not a brilliant response, yet it is the only one I could come up with. Tears dripped down my cheeks. What if Ric had been here? What did those, those... "Assholes!" I pounded my fists into Zach's chest.

Hey," he soothed.

"First, my freakin' boat. Now my freakin' house. What's next?" I gripped a throw pillow so tight my hands are turning white. "What's next? My office or, better yet, my sanity? Oops, too late. I think they got that already tonight!" I let angry words pore out of my mouth.

"Your boat? I didn't get a report on that," Zack inquired. His eyes bore into mine like he's trying to read my mind.

"And why would you?" I screamed. "Why are you even here? I mean, you just mysteriously show up at my front door after someone tries to break in the back!" I sucked in some air. "And why haven't you called me since dinner?" I turned my head, glaring right back. I can look someone in the eye and tell if they are lying. It came in handy in the sales profession and with raising a little boy. I stared, waiting for Zack to speak. Come on, buddy, lie to me so I can scream some more. That would make my day having someone to take all my frustrations out on.

He wiped his hands over his face. "Hmmm, both are good questions," he said in much too calm of a voice. I hated it when authority figures used that voice. In the past, it had always meant I was about to be BS'd. My hand hit the side of my head as it occurred to me, I am screwed.

The silence in the room reverberated, worse than when I was trying to fall asleep earlier. I paused and tried not to flinch, although my legs. I needed to call on my sales skills not to blow this one. This is far more important than any sales situation I'd ever been in. This, after all, is my life.

"OK, you deserve an answer."

"Have you talked with Pete?" he asked as if he already knew I hadn't. This is more of a statement than a question from him.

"No. Why?" I am being harsh, while I placed this bucko under the microscope. I crossed my arms and sat back, leaving a space between our bodies that right away I didn't want. My body language demanded to know what the heck was going on.

But Zack played it cool. He leaned away from me, avoided my gaze, and looked up at the ceiling. He stretched his arms to meet my hands with his, absentmindedly rubbing his thumb against mine. "Pete never returned your call?"

"How do you know, I called Pete?"

"Doesn't matter," Zack answered, sliding over towards me. "Here's what does matter, Max. You're in a situation that has turned dangerous."

"Duh," I said. Give the man credit. He ignored the comment.

"I don't want to scare you, but there are some horrible people in your life right now."

"Present company included?"

"I repeat I can't go into details, but you need to make some decisions. I can tell you the folks doing this done it all before, and they are not people to be messed with…"

Zack shook his head, then continued. "You should know right now there are two choices. You can move to someplace safer, or you can be under twenty-four-hour watch and have an officer or hired gun move in here. Take your pick."

Hired gun? What the heck did I need a hired gun for? They only did that in the movies. Wasn't I a simple girl from the shoreline? Wasn't this a random break-in? This mess had Jon written all over it. That F-in' putz!

I started to speak, but Zack kept ongoing. "Tonight, I have a van coming, and you are going to take anything important to you and load it into the van. Then you are going to move to a condo we have in town until Ric comes back on Sunday."

"I'm going to what? And who's we? Better yet, who are you?" This is all way too much illusion and not enough on the answer side. "I need to call Gert." I leaned over to reach for the phone. Before I had it in my hands, Zack snatched it away.

"You can't call Gert." This is not a request. This is an order.

"Can't call Gert?" No Gert? Gert's my protection. She is my advisor. She knew the law, and she got answers. I wanted to call her. "Why not?"

"I can't answer that. You need to trust me on this. No Gert. You can call Pete or your parents, but no

Gert." Damn. He is not asking me, he is telling me. The room spun, black dots appeared before my eyes, I shook my head in an attempt to gain focus.

"Well,, I would call Pete, but he has this annoying habit of not returning my calls…"

"I can fix that." He watches me freak out.

"And I'm not calling my parents yet because I don't want to worry about them." Or hear them say what a loser Jon is and how I should have known better. Speaking of Jon…

"What about Jon? Can I call Jon?"

"No." Zack moved forward. I am beginning to think that Zach had no other word in his vocabulary. "No, Jon. No Gert. You may only call your parents and Pete. I'll repeat what I said before. Maxi, this is real, what's happening. There are two choices right now. You can come back here with a twenty-four-hour watch when Ric is back in your custody, or you and he can stay at the condo. But until then you can't stay here alone. It's not safe."

"Do you always say no to everything?"

"Not everything." His eyes went dark, and the room got sauna hot. He is being forceful and kind of sexy too. My hand hit the side of my head again. It had been way too long since I'd been with a man. Here sat a guy thinking about saving my life, while I want to jump his bones. Not good.

I took the phone out of Zack's hand and dialed Pete yet again. Freakin' voice mail! I pointed to the phone, so Zack could see it went straight to voice mail, and then without thinking, I spoke at the beep. "Pete, you suck, you rotten bag of dog crap. My house just got broken into. It's four in the morning. Zack Brady from high school is sitting here telling me to leave. It's not safe here." I mimicked Zack's voice in frustration. "I can't call my freakin' lawyer, I can call Mom and Dad, but I don't want to freak them out, and you are not calling me back. Help me regain my sanity!" I slammed the end button and then placed another call. I woke up my sister-in-law and gave her the same nasty message before I threw the phone back to Zack.

"You should be nicer to her," he commented. "She may not give Pete the message."

"Based on past experience, she already forgot it," I answered. "Are my parents and Ric safe?" This is the only thing I cared about right now.

"Yes," he answered.

"How do you know?"

"Trust me."

"For now." I started to pace in my living room. Past the coffee table, my dad had made over to the toy chest spilling over with the Lego parts, game pieces, and Nerf guns. Back to the loveseat, I was supposed to get rid of months ago but couldn't because I used it to fold laundry, and if I got rid of it, I wouldn't have a place for my folded clothes. I plopped down next to a stack of clothes. It promptly tumbled in my direction, and Ric's baseball uniform unfolded. "There are a few things I'll need with me. I'd prefer to stay here, and I would like to talk to my lawyer." My eyes started to water again, and I'd be damned if I'm going to let this guy see me cry twice in one encounter.

"No, Gert," he repeated quietly. "Let's get what you need together and get you out of here." Zack stood and pulled me up into his arms.

He leaned away to pick up the uniform, placing the baseball pants and shirt in the space I had vacated. I marched off in the direction of my office. My eye caught movement through the window. Two officers were pointing at something on my porch. I wobbled my head and sighed. Why me?

Chapter Fourteen

Ok, I admit, I didn't listen to Zach's directions too Well,. After all the excitement at my house, I gave in and let Zack move me, a few boxes of old business records he thought were important enough not to leave in my home, and some personal items, all into one of the condos I had considered buying into. This one overlooked one of the marinas at the point. I try to be positive, looking at this as a rare opportunity to try the real estate before buying it.

From the enormous dome-shaped window on the second floor, I saw lines of yachts and sailboats bobbing in the water. This view would make a lovely future home. With some luck and a few deaths, I'd be able to dock my boat right outside my living room picture window. The massive window would look out onto the bow of my boat, of course, and came complete with a sunset view of the river.

I shook my head in disbelief and went back to the marina across the street. My little Slug Puppy boat could fit inside the living room of any one of the vessels docked out there. They were new, large, sleek, beautiful, and probably started at a million easily. But I could afford one without blinking after I sold my business to Carlson. It wouldn't matter, though. Just looking at those boats made me homesick for mine. My boat, the one with the ugly couch now up for sale because it had been contaminated with sleazy people germs. It struck me I should be on my boat right now, anchored somewhere in the middle of Long Island sound, drinking cosmos in the sunshine, and reading a Nora Roberts novel. But instead, here I sat treated like a prisoner with a view. Life is so unfair.

I keep trying to find something positive in the whole mess. It went with my nature. Ric would love this place, for one thing. We would still be in town, and the complex had a pool. He could bring his buds over to hang out. I try to figure out how I could explain all this to him, but I still hadn't come up with something that would be believable. Hell, I didn't even know what is going on, and I hated lying to my kid, even if the truth would probably scare the poop out of him. I knew that because it is kind of scaring the poop out of me, and I am supposed to be the adult. I could say our house is contaminated with some weird germs, mold spoors, or, better yet, bugs. Yeah, Ric would love it to be bugs. And if it were bugs, he'd know I would be out of there in a flash.

As long as I am dreaming, I could buy this place. Then, after everything is finally settled with Jon, and they caught the sleazeballs who had been invading my space, my life would get back to normal. Normal. What a concept. But no one could tell me when that might be. I held onto myself while glancing back at the boats. I added to my fantasy a new boat with a purple couch, docked across the street. In my imagination, it is all about me, for once in my life.

I am all by myself, without Zack or Ric. I'd feel a lot better if I had him with me over the weekend. Nope, better, he wasn't at the house or anywhere near the turmoil there. I breathed in a sigh of relief he hadn't been in harm's way.

I wondered if going to church might help settle my brain. My left hand reached up and smacked the side of my head. Jon got the church. Well, he didn't actually get the church. He still went once in a while, and with all the gossip hounds around, it would be too uncomfortable for me to even pray there. It is time to find a new church, also.

I walked around, looking for my purse and, more importantly, my cell phone. I found them both on a marble table in the foyer. I opened my address book and hit send. "Brunch, a half-hour at the point," I stated, hanging up before I got an answer. I dropped my phone back into my purse, walked into the bathroom on my right, turned on the faucet, splashed water on my face, and got ready for my great escape.

Chapter Fifteen

        Gert sat across from me, spilling the details of
her date from the previous night. We were at the luxury
inn across the street from the condos. I couldn't drive
anywhere because my car is still parked in my
driveway. Besides, Zach made me a bit paranoid. I
hadn't told Gert where I am staying. Boy, would she be
jealous. I remember she tried to buy one of the units,
but for some odd reason, the association rejected her
application. She was pissed. I never found out why they
didn't want her. I did find out how Gert is accustomed
to getting her way. She threatened to sue. After making
the threat, the whole situation faded away.
        Zack's voice echoed in my head. "No, Gert." My
stomach is doing the flip flop thing. The last time I
didn't listen to my gut, I ended up married to a dirtbag.
Obviously, that didn't turn out too well. Staying at the
condo is about all I plan on not telling her. After what
happened last night, I might need a good lawyer.
        "Can you believe he expected to stay the night
after all that?" She inclined back in her chair, snorting
with laughter.
        I guessed the date hadn't gone too well. I should
be paying attention, but my mind wandered off. I
would love to have a dating story to tell. Actually, I did.
I called Gert to meet me for brunch after I got settled at

the condo. I needed normalcy in my life. We are noshing on fresh greens with basmati vinegar and extra virgin olive oil dressing. But we were not being health conscious. This is our first course. Believe me, there is a lot more food yet to be served.

"What have you been up to? I called the house, and the machine isn't picking up." Elegantly, she raised her fork and stuffed her mouth with salad.

"I've had an interesting weekend," I began. Gert twirled her fork, urging me to continue. "Last night someone tried to break into my house. That was exciting."

"What?" Gert spit a few greens across the table. Her fork dropped. She rushed around the table to throw her arms around me. My fork hit my plate with a loud bang. "You were home? Are you ok? Did they catch the bastards?"

I gulped a deep breath, "Yes, I'm ok, I guess. I'm going to stay somewhere else, but I'm not sure where yet. And no, they didn't catch the guys."

Gert rounded the table back to her seat and her salad, keeping her eyes locked with mine. "Do they know who it was, at least?" Now that is an interesting question. "And why didn't you call me?"

"No clue who. And I would have called but between Zack showing up and the police and such, Well, let's say I wasn't in good thinking form." Staring at my food did not make this easier to re-live again. I held my hands under the table, so she wouldn't see them shake. I shove salad into my mouth, but that didn't help either. I knew the salad tasted good, but I didn't notice. Gert would press for every last detail. That is the lawyer in her.

"You called Zack instead of me?" Oh boy. There's the raised eyebrow again. Hey, there's something she and Nancy had in common.

"I didn't call him. He showed up with the police."

"He just showed up? Maxi, this is not good. How did he know?" Gert took a massive swig of water. "What did you say he does again?"

He saves damsels in distress. "Something for the government. Computers. I don't know." I am pretty sure he broke hearts too, but I hadn't gotten that far yet.

The waitress carried over round two. The beautiful colors of blueberry ricotta crepes, apple pancakes, a spinach potato frittata, and a side of extra crispy bacon spread across our table. The portions were typical French, meaning tiny. The food, however, is cosmic. In silence, we both piled equal pieces on our plates. I savored the sweet tang of the apple pancakes before continuing the conversation.

"Max," Gert did the fork waving thing again, "you need to be careful. I mean, this guy shows up in your life, and then your boat and your house get broken into. What is up with that?"

My mouth moved slow on the pungent sweet combination crepes. "I don't know what's up with that. I need to get in touch with my brother, who currently is not returning my calls so…" What else could I say? Gert did have a point, but at the moment I convinced myself Pete is the missing link or at least a life preserver to hang on to. "I am being careful, and I think I'm being pretty smart sharing what happened with my lawyer." I tried to make light of the situation. Still, even the sweet ricotta filed pancakes smothered in blueberry syrup

142

venturing through my taste buds did not settle my nerves. I should be running on the treadmill instead of noshing. Or ordering more alcohol would do the trick. "When I talk to Pete, I'll need a better idea of what's going on. I think I will break down, call his wife again, and see what's up. Maybe she'll have a clue."

We both started snickering. Blueberry sauce went up Gert's nose. My sister-in-law, as bright as she is academic, had never been very savvy with people. She could compute elaborate math equations in her head but ask her a simple, common-sense question, and it is all too much for her. When she finished a conversation or got frustrated with who she's speaking with, she often left the room or just hung up the phone. In her world, the conversation had ended. It was actually kind of creepy. I only try to reach her when I absolutely had to.

"Yeah, she'll tell you where he is." Gert wiped her nose and repositioned herself in her chair. "Remember the time your dad went into the hospital, and you had to call her to get a hold of Pete?"

"Not a good memory," I said.

"What did she say to you? Oh yeah, I remember. Maxi, dear," Gert imitated Pete's wife's lecture voice, the one she used with her kids and others who irritated her, "You may only contact Pete in an absolute emergency. Like your dad being in intensive care wasn't an emergency."

"The best part was when she added if he died, we shouldn't do anything because Pete can't receive bad news while he's working."

We both sat and shook our heads, smiling at the absurdity of my sister-in-law's mindset. Gert glanced at

143

something over my shoulder, or this could be my imagination. She nodded in the direction of the lady's room and got up. "Hands off my plate," she pointed at her food.

I watch as Gert leaves the room and catch sight of someone who looked like the Tart in the lobby. I wondered what the bimbo would be doing in a place way too classy for the likes of her. Maybe she had an afternoon quickie with another guy. That would serve Jon right. I started snickering aloud at the thought. My soon-to-be ex-husband's new lover caught cheating on him at the most expensive hotel in town. In a town where everyone knew everyone else's business. Imagine! Hillsey and Jon had been the number one gossip topic for about a year now, so it isn't like no one else would notice her prancing around here.

Wiping my watery eyes, I observe a few folks staring in my direction. Quite frankly, I didn't care what strangers think of me. Heck, at this point, I didn't care what people who knew me think about me!

What would you do if your business were in chaos? I would make a list of the reasons for it. Then I'd take the list and get organized. I hit myself on the side of the head.

"Duh, Maxi." I didn't know why, but having a list makes me feel better, especially when I could cross off my accomplishments. I reach for my purse on the floor, pull out a pen, and a half-used memo pad. Opening the pad, I write #1 on the top of the page and continue to number down the side until I reached ten. I start at the beginning: dog breath meeting, then Zack, then Jon, then Bob Carlson.

Carlson's name caused a head slap, I forgot all about him. I hadn't accepted his offer, and the deadline passed. Crap! "Need to call immediately," I write in parentheses next to his name. I continue down the list: boat people, house alarm, Zack again, PETE in all caps because the putz hadn't called me back yet. What else am I missing? There is something more. But what?

"Sorry. Took longer than I thought." Gert slid back into her chair. "What are you doing?"

"I am making a list of things I need to get done and the events of the last few days, so I can try to figure them out." I slip the memo pad and pen back into my purse.

"Figure what out? Max, I am here to organize, streamline, and legalize, remember?" Gert attempted to grab for my purse, but I knocked it into my lap.

"And you are so good at doing all those things," I said. "Almost as good as these apple pancakes." I shove a forkful in my mouth and grin. The little voice inside my head now sounding more like Zach, reminds me to be careful. Gert is fishing. Or could it be possible I have observed her too many times with clients, and I am over Virgo-ing all this. Zack had made me paranoid.

I concentrated on my half of the spinach frittata. Gert slowly sipped her water. The silence forming between us didn't feel right.

"I'll call you first next time," I blurted out. Gert smiled, but the smile didn't reach her eyes. "We need to talk about the sale," I changed the subject. "I've decided to move forward." With that comment, my casual brunch billable time.

Chapter Sixteen

After leaving the inn, I told Gert I should walk the point awhile to clear my head and work off what we devoured. When I looked out at the water, the swirling thoughts in my brain became organized. Something about the salty smell and flickers of white light along the surface put my mind into a sorting mode. As a kid, I thought the flashes of light were fairies dancing on the surface, protecting me from bad things. Those damn fairies are slacking off lately.

One of my friends is an editor at a fishing magazine. He had his office changed so he wouldn't space out the window watching the boats. I need to space out to organize; otherwise, my life would be even more of a mess.

I sat down on a bench that smelled like greasy fried clams, and I pulled out my list. I started to consider the changes I had encountered over the past few months. Jon is gone, with Hillsey, bimbo of the year. Because of our slow antiquated court system, they were currently sharing custody of Ric with me. Even though things had not settled, I felt like this part is okay, or if not okay, it is not entirely idiotic. Ric deserved to see his father, even if I thought the man was a complete imbecile. Besides, I know Jon would never consciously do anything to hurt Ric. In his own warped way, he loved his son.

In the past week, both of my sanctuaries, my boat, and my home had been violated to the point where I am too scared to be at either. Of course, I would never admit I had a weakness there. I thought I needed to leave both behind. If I had really wanted to, I could relate everything back to Jon, since I knew he wanted a piece of everything I owned. Eventually, I would need to sell both even if I there wasn't some wacko breaking in. Sooner or later, this all has to go. Everywhere I turned in the house or on the boat, it would eventually remind me of Jon. Then I'd get nostalgic, breakdown, and decide to sell and start over. Today, however, I am feeling like a vindictive bitch. She is unwilling to do anything that might make my ex wealthier. In the end, I figured he would probably get what he wants, no matter what I do.

One sad part about it all is living in a small town, and shy of taking out a full-page ad in the local weekly proclaiming my innocence, I had become a hot topic of the rumor mill, something I always tried to avoid.

A big cigarette boat droned by. It looked like the same boat I had seen a few days ago. I watched it pass and wondered why anyone would want such an obnoxious craft. Down in the Keys, one of my buddies used to call them drug runner boats. Whenever I saw one, I can't help wondering what the cargo is.

A dead ringer for Hillsey is sitting on the lounge chair in back, boobs bopping with the waves. Seeing this duplicate in a bathing suit is a reminder of why Jon left. Well,, one of many reasons. I still found it hard to believe he could be so shallow, but then again, I should know better. He was always surrounded by lost loose-looking women on tour, acting like a big man on campus at every venue. I guessed that it was part of his attraction. He was cool.

I reached up and hit the side of my head with my left hand. UGH! I got to stop beating myself up all the time!

The whirling sound of a strained engine brought me back. Another person on the lounge looked familiar too. I couldn't tell because I am looking at her back, but still… I tried to shake out the cobwebs. I needed to concentrate on the task at hand, not stare at Well,-built women on hundred-thousand-dollar boats.

I review my notes on the house, the boat, and the business. Even though I already made the decision to sell, I am still not sure it is the right choice. It made the most comfortable choice. Since February, when all the crap with Jon started, I hadn't been into growing the company. I stopped looking into any new markets. Heck, I had hired a temp up in Boston. Boston, a million-dollar territory, and I trusted it to someone who didn't even work for me.

Well,, I signed her paychecks, although they were made out to a third party. I could sell all the publications off as franchises and take in royalty fees. What am I thinking? I had already accepted Bob Carlson's offer. The real question is: What should I do after my contract is up? I'd need to do something. I am only in my forties.

This is a good sign. I am back to planning. I just believed my life could become normal again. When would it be normal again, I didn't know, but I thought it would happen. Maybe this is the right time to work for someone else again. Ric and I could even move out west somewhere. We could live in the mountains, and I could be a director of sales and marketing at some five-star ski resort. Ric would go to their academy, learn from professionals, and live the kind of life kids dream of. Or, better yet, I could become a ski bum too. You know, bartend during the day and on weekends and holidays, and then ski like mad during the slow weeks. I could get Jon to sign over full custody. Right. And pigs would fly.

I pick my cell out of my purse and press numbers I should have forgotten long ago. It's the weekend, so I get a voice mail. I hit the pound sign to bypass Bob Carlson's secretary's voice. "Hey Bob, it's Maxi. I know my deadline was Friday, but I had a few things come up. If the offer still stands, we should talk. I'd like to move forward, pending a few changes to the agreement. I appreciate your flexibility, and I look forward to talking soon." Ok. I had made up my mind. I took action.

I hear snippets of conversations as I walk along the banks, looking at the beautiful river's mouth open by the lighthouse. The rush at the end of the river pushed the boaters into Long Island Sound.

A couple walked by holding hands. "Oh, wow. Honey, look at the birds."

They were young and obviously in love. She is so thin she would be lost if she stood sideways, wearing tight lime short shorts and a halter top that matched her sandals. Her jet-black hair is tied up into a ponytail that bounced while she walked. Her arm draped around a tall, athletic guy with a receding hairline. He had a nice body, but she could do better. I saw a beer gut in his future, plus he was going to go bald before he turned thirty. The way he moved screamed, "Look at me!" yet he had slacker written all over him. I had experience with slackers and could tell these things.

"Aren't they cute?" she cooed.

"Cute. Babe, those are seagulls, man. All they do is squawk and shit."

Boy, I am eavesdropping on Mister Romantic. But Ms. Ponytail is looking at him like he just gave her the keys to the Benz. There *is* a butt for every seat, as they said in the car biz.

A little farther down, I spotted the elderly couple I had met a few days earlier. They were taking up space on one of the benches. She knitted and he, Well, I couldn't tell what he was doing, but whatever it was, he did it. Well,. His hand rested on his stomach, and his eyes appeared half-closed. His wife jabbered at him happily while her hands move gracefully. I hoped they don't see me. That is all I need. "Edmund, isn't that the weird lady from last week over there?" "Sure is, Ethel. Don't talk to her or offer her any lifesavers. She might come over." I shuttered at the thought as I walked around the pavilion, out of their sight range.

Through the pavilion windows, I could see a yoga class in progress. The instructor gave directions, and although I couldn't hear what she is saying, she must be projecting a calm spell on all those who chose to attend her class. I should take a yoga class. I could use a calming spell, and I could walk here from my new temporary quarters. Yeah, walk to yoga class, float back home.

I find myself watching and moving with the class. When their right arms rise above their heads, mine moves too. They lean over to stretch the right side of their bodies, and so do I. Raising my left arm, I repeat the stretch. What a great place to give a class. I need to make time and actually be an attendee. The yogi's unfolded their mats. As they lay down, the room became quiet and serene. I could barely hear the soft music, a spacey Egyptian sound.

Maybe all I need is to venture down to the health food store on Main and buy a new age CD. That might do the trick. I glimpsed back past the parking lot towards the condos and caught Zack standing on the deck. If I didn't know better, I'd say he's watching me.

I move the pebbles on the ground with my feet. What was it about Gert at brunch today? My hand flew up, stopping short of my head. I hadn't told Gert about the boat vandals. "Oh my god!" Yet she had said something about my boat getting broken into. How did she know?

I looked back, and Zack had disappeared. I imagined he is pacing inside, trying to decide if he should just let me die in my house or if he needed to help someone who couldn't (or wouldn't) follow directions. Who cared if he dumps me! I am not a teenager anymore. I am a mature woman. Heck, I had just been dumped by my husband of ten years, so why not by a crush from high school? Realistically, what did it all matter anyway?

"I care," I said aloud. I went back to the view of the inn and the boats. I didn't want to care. I want this whole mess over with. In a year or so, I could be open to a new relationship, but not now. That would be dumb on my part.

I watch Zack cross the street, moving towards me. He is casual in jeans and a polo shirt. His hair covered with a baseball cap. As he got closer, I saw his cap had a B on the front. I take a quick look over at the yoga class. The participants are coming out of their trances.

"Decided to take a walk?" Gosh, he moved quickly. One minute he stood on the other side of the parking lot and the next beside me. "I thought you were going to stay in and get organized."

I couldn't put my finger on it, but something told me he is pissed. Maybe it is how his hands rest on his hips or the fire in his eyes. Either way, I could feel a lecture coming on.

"It's such a gorgeous day. Who wants to work?" I tried to smile back.

"Is that why you own your own business, Maxi, so you can play hooky when you want?"

He pretended to be relaxed, but I could feel the tension. His jaw tightened as he gazed out at the river, obviously distracted by one of the vessels crowding its way back upstream. He took his hat off, held it with one hand while finger, and combed his hair back in place with the other. God, he had great hair. The little voice inside my head begged my heart not to fall. Then I remember it is too late.

"Yeah, one of the reasons. But think about it, Zack," I said, as my eyes darted from the Red Sox logo on his hat to his face. "If I worked for somebody else, I never would have known someone broke into my boat because I would be in an office instead...."

"And this would be a bad thing?" His lips curved into a sexy smile. Is that a joke? Maybe he is not as upset as I thought.

"I guess the corporate world has its advantages. I mean, I could be having to take personal time today to be here instead of…Zack, it's the weekend. I wouldn't be working anyway." He laughed. "So what brings you here? Playing tourist?" I asked.

"Not exactly. See, I'm trying to help a friend out. People keep breaking into her house, boat, and office space…"

"Office? They broke into my office? When?"

"…and I want to know why." He gently rubbed his hand along my arm. He gave the same look at the house. I started to feel dizzy. The black spots danced around me again.

"Best estimate is it was sometime today. Not sure of the time but we got the call around 1 pm your door was wide open."

"One, today?"

Zack nodded and sauntered towards the rail. He leaned back against it, looking out into space. Seagulls gathered to one side, hoping we would sit and eat some food they could beg for. The salt air grew heavy, and my gourmet started to make an encore appearance.

Strange things keep happening. Unless psychics surround me, there are far too many coincidences and weird events taking place, like Gert with my boat, or Zack with my business. It struck me as the owner of the company I should have been the one notified, not this almost stranger standing next to me.

"How come I wasn't called?" My teeth clenched. I try to keep my emotions in check.

"The police called the condo and got an answering machine. So, the sergeant on duty had my card and called me."

Okay, that sounded like a rational explanation.

"I called the condo and got the machine, so I checked up on Ric, who is fine by the way, and went to your office. I figured you would turn up sooner or later. Obviously, listening and following directions is not one of your strong suits."

I didn't say anything. Instead, I counted to one hundred in my head. I do that with my brothers a lot since they know what buttons to push. Right now, Zack had pushed all of them and then hit the bright red emergency button when he mentioned Ric.

"You checked up on Ric? What made you do that?"

"I was worried, but he's okay. He is over at Rye's house playing with a bunch of boys."

"Rye's house?" I clench my fists at my side. "He is supposed to be hanging out with his father, not his buds. It's not like Jon spends a ton of time with him. You'd think when he has the opportunity, he would want to see his kid. I mean, come on, what father doesn't want to spend time with his kid? Hello. If he was going to be at Rye's house, he could spend the weekend with me. It certainly wouldn't matter either way."

"MAXI!"

I guess I began to go off on a tangent. Zack's shouting my name got my attention along with everyone else within earshot.

"Maxi, calm down. All that matters is Ric is safe."

He was right, although since he's a man, I would never admit it. "Really? And where pray tell, is Ric's father?" I crossed my arms and faced away.

"Somewhere out there," Zack pointed towards the river. "He's on a boat with friends; at least that's what his girlfriend's daughter said. They were in the house by themselves when I stopped by earlier."

I open my mouth to say something as Zack's lips turn up into a smile.

"I already called DCF, and they are investigating. I requested they send a copy of the report to you directly along with a second copy to your lawyer's office. I assume that would still be Lenora G. O'Hara?"

"Lenora G. O'Hara? Who is that? My lawyer's name is Gert Fontaine."

"Lenora Gertrude O'Hara is your lawyer's legal name. Maxi, I told you to be careful. How much did you share with her at brunch?"

Crap, he knew about the brunch. "Not much, but she shared something with me," I said, standing a little taller.

"And what would that be?" Zack had his arms crossed over his chest and offered up that killer smile of his. Boy, if we had gotten together under different circumstances—even though I still hadn't figured why we were together now if we were together now. I thought about giving up. The sad part is Zach dumping me would probably hurt more than Jon leaving me.

"She knew about the boat."

Zack's smile froze. I wish I knew him better so I could read his mind.

"Zack, did you hear me?" I repeated, "She knew about the boat!"

"I heard you, Max. I just don't know what to say." Something in the distance caught his eye, and he took my hand in his. "Let's go back to the condo and figure this thing out."

"What about Ric? He's supposed to come back tomorrow."

"We'll pick him up at Rye's at five. If Jon's shipping him off to his friends, he won't know the difference, right?"

I nodded.

"We will keep it all legal and create a paper trail, so there are no questions later on."

I allow Zack to lead me back towards the condo complex. I liked the feeling of his hand in mine way more than I should.

Chapter Seventeen

I walked right past the entrance to the condo. My car has mysteriously appeared in a space in the last row. I head straight to it. I need to see what my office looks like, and I am debating on picking up Ric at his friend's house. I fumble through my purse, dropping tampons, gum, my wallet, and other contents on the ground as I aggressively search for my keys. The car next to me beeped.

I jumped up to see Zack getting in. He reaches over to open the passenger door. I didn't even notice his car.

In silence, we drive down Main Street towards my office. It took less than five minutes. Zach parks next to Nancy's corvette.

"Those sons of bitches," I hear her yelling as we enter the building. "Those sons of bitches!"

My office looked like an indoor hurricane had blown through. Files scattered everywhere. All of Nancy's cabinets emptied onto the floor. Whoever broke in was looking for something. I wonder what they were looking for and whether or not they found it.

I walk through Nancy's area to my office. I didn't think it could get worse, but I am wrong again. My files are emptied all over the floor, along with all the mugs that sat on my desk, holding pens, pencils, paper clips, etc. There is something brown oozing on the walls. It could be graffiti, although it didn't say anything, at least not anything I could read.

My wall safe stood wholly exposed but not open. The monitor to my computer lay smashed on the floor. There is stuff everywhere. I inhale a deep breath and shake my head to create a sea of little black dots. I am speechless. Fortunately, I could hear Nancy swearing enough for the two of us. I must say, she did have a way with words.

"Maxi, I know this is premature asking you this, but do you notice anything missing?" Zack rested against the doorway with his arms across his chest.

"Hey, Nance, Zack here would like to know if we are missing anything." I tried to keep a straight face. Nancy looked up at me, wide-eyed like I had grown a second head.

"What?" she replied. I could see she is getting ready to blow again.

I attempt to keep my voice calm and rational. "Oh, and did you seen the Newport file?"

Nancy stared up at me like she is ready to kill. Her eyes are glossy and mean.

"Just kidding," I add before bursting into tears.

"The freaking file is right here," Nancy said, pointing to the pile on the floor. "Freaking dirtbags did this. I can't believe someone would do this to us. I mean, come on, Max, we are nice people. We treat folk the right way. When I get my hands on whoever did this, they will rue the day. I am going to kick their butts clear up to the state jail in Danbury. Then I'm going to call my cousin who works there and ask if they could be tortured or at least hooked up with the biggest badass dude he can find. Know what I mean? Creating work for me is not a good thing to do." Nancy breathed in deep, then looked over at me. I giggled. Only she could put everything in perspective.

"Thank you," I said through the tears. Nancy continued to pick up papers, trying her best to organize it all. God bless her.

"Is there any way to tell what's missing?" Zach repeated.

Nancy answered promptly. "It's all backed up on the computer. Maxi insists on having paper copies too." She rolled her eyes in my direction.

"You have it on your hard disc...."

"And back-up discs. In my home safe. I keep everything," I replied. "Oh, and I had some on the boat too, but I moved them."

"Where to?" I point to the wall safe, and he grinned. Nancy rolled her eyes again and went back to picking up papers.

"Nancy is right, though. Most of what I have is crap I keep because I am paranoid. We would be looking for a needle in a haystack."

"What do you want to do with all this, Max?" Nancy inquired from behind her desk.

I looked around at the mess, thinking I want to burn it all. Zack must have read my mind.

"Since you have a digital back up, you can throw it all out. I would call one of those shredder companies to get this all destroyed." Zack strolled around my office, picking up papers at random. "Let's take your hard drive back to the condo. I can call in a computer expert." He had one hand in his front pocket while the other continued to pick up papers at random.

His eyes darkened. I noticed, for the first time, the dark shadows underneath. "I need to make a call."

I watched him walk out the door. Man, he had a nice butt.

"I know what you are thinking, and although I agree, I don't understand your priorities." Mother Nancy said. I swear she scares me sometimes.

I ignored her and continue to pick up papers. "Oh, the hell with it!" Papers fly through the air. I turn into a madwoman, throwing stuff, knocking whatever the burglars left on my desk onto the floor, as I scream, "I can't believe I am letting someone take over my life. WHAT THE FUDGE IS GOING ON!!!"

My rampage continued as a file gave me a paper cut across my left hand. Trickles of blood slid onto everything I grabbed. I left pieces of me. Sweat equity I had poured into making my business work for three years—sweat equity in making a marriage work that had failed miserably. I wanted to scream.

Everything around me blurred together. "I want my life back!" I kick my desk, hard, with my Birkenstocks. What a dumb move on my part. Pain shoots up my leg. I crash to the floor. Nancy and Zack are standing in the doorway, watching me. "I want my life back." Both nodded in unison. "I want my freaking life back now!" I scream.

Nancy helped me up, steering me towards the restroom. She bandaged my hand, washed my face, and handed me a clean towel. "You still thinking about retirement?" she asked, again reading my mind.

"Yeah. Don't know if it will help, though. I mean these people," I threw my arm up in the air, "have hit my house, my boat, and now my office. Who are these jerk faces, and what do they want from me?"

Nancy shrugged. For once, she didn't have the answers. We joined Zack in the lobby. I needed to call a shredder company, get this mess cleaned up, re-establish a sense of order, and, after all that, I am going to run away and hide.

Chapter Eighteen

Zack sat in the living room, talking on the phone. I couldn't see him. All I can hear is, "Okay, I understand. That should be the logical next step." Nothing he said made much sense. He is speaking in terms too general for me to interpret.

I drank a cup of green tea. Back at the condo, I had been staring at the marina for an hour. My body bent across a chair, and my legs dangled over the side. Every few seconds, I swayed one leg to release nervous energy.

Gert had left a message on my cell phone, reminding me we were scheduled for another meeting with the dynamic duo. Oh, joy.

"Is that your version of exercise?" Zack asked.

"Huh?" I watched him walk but hadn't heard a word he said.

"Forget it." Zack sat on the floor in front of me. The blue sky from the window surrounded him, and I could see sailboat masts peeking up behind his shoulders. "I have an idea," he said. "You, me, dinner?" He raised and lowered his eyebrows like Groucho Marx in the old Marx Brother Movies.

"Like we both need to eat dinner, or we're having a date dinner?" I ask. He is so adorable sitting there in his Dockers and golf shirt. In the case of Zack

Brady verses, Maxi Malloni's heartbreak seemed inevitable. I guess the only questions left were when and to what degree.

I bit my lower lip and waited for his answer. I must be off the wall, to crave a romantic date.

Zack laughed at me. "What would you like it to be, Max?" He shifted over to lean up against the window frame. The tips of his hair picked up select rays of sunshine streaming into the room. My face grew warm, but my nauseous pit calmed.

"Oh, shoot!" I looked over, and Zack raised his eyebrows. "I'd like to go to dinner with you," I stated firmly.

My inner voice continued, *then I'd like to spend the night with you, but saying this aloud would make me kind of slutty, so we'll skip it and go back to the question I didn't answer.*

"Good. That's settled. We can figure out what and where later." Zack ran his right hand over his head, resting it on top. "There is something else I need to talk to you about. It could wait until later, but it would probably make our evening less relaxing."

I move my neck back to view the ceiling fan. I inhale deeply, hold it, and then let a slow breath out. I try to remember if my horoscope had said anything about me having a breakdown today. "We should talk about it now then," I sigh. Whatever it is, I might as well, get it over with, and anything less than him still being married or confessing gay couldn't possibly faze me. I'd been through enough in the past few weeks.

"I have a proposition for you," he started.

I shift to sit taller in the chair. Dude, proposition me all you want.

"I'm listening," I said, oh so coolly.

"Okay. I believe we are in a situation here that has the potential to go in a lot of directions." Zack stretched his legs out. "Would you agree?"

I slip out of the chair to sit on the floor. I stretch my legs out alongside his. "I agree." How could I not agree? The hairs on my thighs stood at attention, giving off little electric zings in his direction.

"My experience with this has been to lean more to the side of caution. I think we need to take every opportunity to be safe. This condo," he lifted his arms up with a sweeping motion, "for example, is a safe place."

I nod my head waiting for him to continue. "So, Max, I think you should stay here to be safe and help facilitate catching the scum who are wreaking havoc on your life. But, I also think Ric would be a distraction to you during all this."

He hit me with a figurative brick. "What do you mean a distraction?" I started getting peeved he referred to my kid in the negative.

"I guess I used the wrong words. I think you would be concerned about Ric and that has the potential to put both of you in unnecessary danger. Like most mothers, I sense you may be a bit overprotective of him."

"I can admit at times I have been known to be a bit overprotective with my child." It sounded like I was defending myself on trial. Jon had pulled me in more than once for what he considered coddling Ric. I guess it is my tendency as a mother. I carried him around inside me, and I still wanted to protect him.

"Without being out of line or too blunt, I think Ric would be safer somewhere else, say on vacation with his grandparents. Pete actually suggested that one." He said this so innocently he didn't pick up he said the wrong thing until after it came out.

"You talked to Pete?" Now I am getting aggravated all over again. "When?" Zack could get my no good, rotten piece of decaying food on the sidewalk, brother to call him back, but for his own flesh and blood, he is too busy? Horse manure!

"We talked after your house incident. That's when he suggested things might get worse before they get better. Pete is more familiar with this kind of thing than I am." Zack looked everywhere but in my direction. Unconsciously I enrolled him in the scumbag club with the rest of the male population in the universe.

"So, I am to understand my brother has talked to you directly, in person, regarding what's happened in my life, yet he hasn't spoken about it with me?" I fumed.

Zack held his hands out in front of him, peace offering style. "Okay, Max. Let me explain. I at least owe you that."

"At least…" My arms crossed so tightly my chest actually hurt. "You know, Zack, you say that, yet I'm not getting any explanations."

"Pete is working on something highly sensitive. I don't know all the details of his project. Still, I do know he is worried sick about you and is trying to help find out why these people are breaking into your space, whoever they are, and, most importantly, what they want. He's doing this in addition to his job. And I'm sure whatever Uncle Sam has him working on is something important to our country." Zack's voice grew louder. "I know being swamped is no excuse, but I'm here trying to help with all that along with keeping you safe. That's all I can explain right now." Zack sucked in a huge breath. "I hope this doesn't come out wrong when I say I think Ric needs a vacation away from here. It shouldn't be longer than a week."

"I already talked to my parents about taking him this coming week. I have to get Jon's okay since we share custody." Zack had mentally punched me in the stomach.

"Screw Jon," Zack retorted with a toss of his hand. "I've had enough of his crap. He ships Ric off on weekends as it is. Changing the subject," he leaned in towards me, "I have a place in the White Mountains, nothing fancy. It's an older resort the government inherited due to a huge unpaid tax bill about ten years ago. We actually spent money on it and converted the main house into a lodge. The building sits on a freshwater lake and has great mountain views. There is a full staff to take care of guests. You know, chef, maid, security..."

I waited for more details. The security part made me nervous and relaxed at the same time. "What is this place exactly?"

"It's a retreat. The military uses it for officer getaways, while other branches hold meetings and small conferences there. Sometimes it houses people waiting to testify on our behalf."

I got a chill on that last one.

Zack quickly added, "Scheduled for next week is a retired general taking his grandkids for a quiet getaway. There will be kids Ric's own age to play with, and your parents will have folks to play cards and socialize with too."

Silence. In sales, the rule is the first person who speaks loses. I attempt to process all the information Zack gave me while hoping he would give out a little more. I finally gave up on the latter.

"What if I say no?" I refold my arms the opposite way.

"Well,, that would complicate things. If you decide against this, then I'm not sure what our next steps would be." He spoke in his professional voice. The same one he used on the phone earlier, the strong cop voice. "I do know under the current circumstances I would have to place you and Ric under twenty-four-hour watch and limit you leaving this area."

"I'm sorry, but how would that be different?"

"Good question, Maxi. It would be different in that you wouldn't be going to your office—nor would Nancy—and you certainly would not have the capability to sneak out and meet Gert again. You and Ric would be...here, inside, no pool or outdoor activities." Zack gestured around the room. "Stuck watching soap operas all day long."

"Ewe! So, if I agree to this, Zack and my parents get shipped off to New Hampshire, what do I get?"

"You get to go to work and do in town activities. Pretend your life is normal. I can't let you out on the boat since we are still looking for clues there, and I'm not entirely sure it's safe. This is my own opinion, Max."

He waited for an answer, and this is a tough call. Of course, I wanted to do what is best for my family, yet selfishly I wanted them around to make me feel better. If I said no, it screamed me being self-centered!

"As a bonus, you get to hang out with me for a week," he added with a tired smile.

"Bonus, huh? Zack, all this crap started right after you came into my life."

"Now wait a minute, Maxi. You were in the middle of the Jon situation long before I came here." Zack's body assumed the same position as mine with arms folded, trying to appear more relaxed.

"There weren't creeps breaking in all around me!" I said, quite loud.

"They would be here anyway, and you'd be stuck having to rely on local law enforcement to solve this case." He blew out air. "Maxi, I'm on your side, and I hate to tell you this, but you need me."

He was right, of course, but that didn't make it suck any less. My original plan to get rid of Jon, and not need anyone went out the window. Now I had this old infatuation burning a hole in me.

"Like I have a choice here! I'll call my mom now and explain. When do they need to leave?" My knees cracked as I stood. My purse sat on the chair in the other room. I walked out, grabbed it, pulled out my cell, and walked back in, then leaned against the doorframe. Zack hadn't moved.

He didn't say anything, so I turned on my phone and hit "M" and send. A few seconds later, my father's voice came on the line.

"Hello, Mary Alexis," he answered. My dad got a kick out of caller I.D. sometimes.

"Hello, Daddy," I tried not to cry. "Can you and Mom still take Ric next week? I need to…"

"Yeah, I know. Pete called earlier." I couldn't believe what I was hearing. Freakin' Pete!

"Excuse me, Pete, my brother, called you?" My left foot tapped, and I put on my version of the squinty-eyed tough girl because Zack is looking at me all wide-eyed.

"Yes, your brother Pete. Who else?" Sometimes my dad talked to me as if I were an idiot. "He called and said he got a deal on this rental in the mountains, and were we interested in using it?" Then he added, "What with the house and boat getting broken into you have a lot on your mind, so he suggested we might want to take Ric too."

"He did, did he?" Now my brother is trying to run my life long distance. How many men were going to do this to me? I sucked in air and try to continue conversing in a civilized manner. "You know, it doesn't matter." I wave my hand in the air — my version of regrouping. "So, Dad, do you and Mom want to take my kid for the week?" I couldn't believe how rude I sounded.

"Yeah, sure, as I said, Pete thought that would be a good idea. We're leaving tomorrow afternoon, so can you drop him by?"

Freakin', Pete again! My left hand slapped the side of my head so loud Zack jumped. He must think I am a psycho. I mouth to him, "See what my family does to me?"

Wow, what a position I had put myself in. But really, what choice did I have? I would be a bad mother for not protecting my kid if I didn't let him go. "I could do that. I'll be up around noon." I said it slowly, so I'd remember this wasn't a nightmare. This is my life. My dad said something I didn't catch. "Thanks, Dad!"

I pressed the end and met Zach's gaze. "Can we take a rain check on dinner until tomorrow night? I'd like to spend tonight with my kid." My eyes began to water as I did my best to hold my rolling feelings in.

"No problem, Max," Zack answered. He pushed himself off the floor, sauntered over, and put his arms around me. He circled me into a, "I'm here for you," hug versus a romantic hug. Of course, under the circumstances, he made the perfect move.

"Thanks." I looked up at him and gave a weary smile.

Chapter Nineteen

"Ric, honey, did you pack a toothbrush?"

"For the hundredth time, Mom, YES! And I packed clean underwear and my bathing suit and everything you told me to last night. And guess what? Now it's all in Zack's truck!"

Zack volunteered to drive Ric and me to my parents' up Route 9. It is another beautiful beach day, perfect one might say, with bright sunshine, eighty degrees, light breeze off the water. Traffic backed up with cars heading south, filled with people ready to spend a relaxing day by the pool. For me, it might as well be a hurricane outside.

I hoped this would go smoothly, but it didn't. Ric decided to act like a teenager with a tremendous attitude. He proceeded to push all my buttons, and I knew I would spend the rest of the day, feeling guilty for leaving him with my parents. The sad part is when I call to check up on him, he will most likely be having a blast in his new surroundings. His life would be perfect. And it should be — he's a kid.

The situation reminded me of when he was three, and I'd dropped him at preschool. He would cry elephant tears, scream, and hold on to my leg. "Mommy, don't leave me here!" I would go and cry my eyes out while driving to work. Then I'd call the school about an hour later, and they would tell me he was fine and had been playing with his friends since I left. I actually snuck back one day to peek in the window. There he sat giggling, having a grand old time while his mom suffered from the guilt.

That day the guilt stopped, at least as far as preschool was concerned. In the current situation, I had more than guilt going on. Fear mixed in. I am scared for Ric and my parents and Nancy and my brother and Zack. I am afraid for everyone around me.

"Okay, Ric. I want to check. You know, I forget sometimes." I tried to make peace.

Ric reached around my seat and hugged me from the back.

"It's cool, Mom. When are we getting to Gram and Pops' place?" His arms slid away.

"Soon," I answer, although it would be much too soon for me. I glance over at Zack. He concentrated on driving, not paying attention, yet I think he heard the whole exchange. Zack isn't one to miss much.

"We're in Middletown," Zack said. "I'd say you'll be on your way in less than a half-hour." He turned the radio to a loud rock station. He and Ric bobbed their heads to the beat. Great, now I had two of them. Jon's annoying music habit was singing at the top of his lungs to every Dead song that came on. Unfortunately, Jon couldn't sing, nor had he learned the words to the songs. It was aggravating unless we were in public, then it was just embarrassing.

"So, what are you guys going to do?" Ric asked. "Chase down the bad guys?" I got a chill.

"Nope. Not us. We are staying far away from bad guys," Zack answered.

172

"Good, because I don't want to worry." Then he started laughing, and Zack joined in.

"Am I the brunt of this joke?" I inquire in my proper mother voice.

"Yep," Ric said, laughing louder. His feet moved to the beat, stretched out upon the armrest between the seats. I am tempted to push them back in the back, but it didn't seem to bother Zack, so I let him be.

We arrive at my parents' house fifteen minutes late. A substantial black SUV with government plates was parked in front of my dad's garage, blocking his car in. The back door wide open.

"Just leave your backpack here, Ric. I'll load it," Zack said as he parked next to the other vehicle.

"Thanks. Cool ride," Ric exclaimed, getting out of the car and walked around the SUV before entering the garage. Zack threw his pack in the back, which is already packed with my parents' suitcases, two coolers, and my dad's briefcase. Knowing my dad, the briefcase contained playing cards, chips, a video poker game, a video blackjack game, granola bars, and spare change.

We walk through the garage, around my mom's car, to enter the house through the family room. My mom and dad were talking to some guy in a blue suit with a buzz cut.

"Oh, you're finally here," my dad rose from his chair. "I need to hit the head before we go."

Zack walked over, first shaking hands with my dad then with the suit dude. "Maxi, this is Trent O'Brien. Trent and I work together."

Trent reached out to shake my hand. "It is nice to meet you, Maxi. I've heard a lot about you from Zack here and your brother Pete. Pete and I worked on a few projects together."

"Well,, don't believe everything you hear," I said, adding. "It's nice meeting you too."

"Hey, Zack, got a minute?" Trent inclined his head towards the door. The two disappeared into the garage.

"Maxi, what have you gotten yourself into?" My mom's best personality trait is she always got straight to the point. "That Trent fella is with the FBI. Pete told us he'll be driving us up to New Hampshire." She watched me. I could tell she is trying to catch me lie just like when I was a teenager. "What is going on?"

"Mom, damned if I know," I answer. "I think somehow all of this is tied to my divorce from Jon. I'm not sure how, though." I point with my thumb to the garage. "You and Dad seem to know more than me because of Pete…"

She held her hand up, cutting me off. "Maxi cut your brother some slack. He's working on something for our government. He's busy, you know."

"Yeah, so?"

"Yeah, so that means his job comes first. He sent Zack." I didn't know he sent Zach! "So, someone is watching out for you, and we'll watch out for Ric. From what they tell me, this should all be over in two weeks at the most." Mom paced between the kitchen and the family room. "I wish your father would hurry up. He always has to wait until the last minute, and you know how long he spends in the bathroom."

"Mom, what do you mean, Pete sent Zack?" I got her to stop pacing.

"It means that Zack and Pete worked together, and you know Zack, and Well,, everything will get cleared up." She exited into the kitchen. "I'm going to get your father moving."

As soon as my dad walked back into the room, everything moved quickly. We hugged, I hugged Ric, and they all piled into the big black SUV and waved out the tinted windows as the vehicle moved up the driveway then down the road, out of sight.

I turned to Zack, who is leaning against the car, observing me. "I have a few questions."

He silently walked over and rested his arm across my shoulders, turning my body to lead me back to the passenger door. "I've told you all I can," he answered as he opened the door for me.

"Okay. One question, please," I beg. I brace my arms on top of the door before getting in.

"I will give you one question. But I can't guarantee an answer."

I nod. "Are you working on something for my brother, and did he send you here?"

"That's two questions, Max. First one, yes, I am working on something for your brother and number two, no, he did not send me to see you. As I said the first night we went out, I was looking up an old friend. The rest of this is all coincidence."

I nod and slip into the car. The only satisfaction I am going to get would be from speaking with Pete. Unfortunately, Pete seemed to call everyone back except me. Freakin' Pete!

Chapter Twenty

"Are you almost ready to roll?" Zack stood outside my bedroom door. I guess I took longer to get ready. I keep looking at myself in the mirror, standing in my bra and panties, waiting for the divine inspiration of the outfit. In other words, I couldn't decide what to wear or, to be honest, if I even wanted to go out.

"Give me five." A bunch of clothes are piled on the bed. The last time Zack and I had a date, I went out and bought a new dress. Tonight, all I have are used clothes to wear.

I close my eyes then reach into the pile. I feel the softness of each fabric before I pull one out. With one eye still closed, I peek. In my hand is the lime green sundress I bought to match my Birkenstocks of the same color. Unfortunately, the shoes are back in my house. Zack, like most men, would probably freak if I asked him to go pick up the pair. And if he didn't, I'd wonder about him.

I put the dress back in a pile and pulled out the same tank style in basic dull black. At least my shoes would match. I threw the dress over my head, slipped on my sandals, and evaluated the results in the mirror. With a quick fluff of my hair, I am ready to go.

Taking a deep breath, I opened the door. Zack rested against the windows looking out over the marina.

"I'm ready," I sing out, sounding a bit too happy.

He gave me the staredown. I could feel his eyes move from my head to my toes and back again. I hate when guys do this.

"Wow," he is staring. "You look awesome." I worry about Zack being a good BSer, and worse yet, I keep falling for his lines.

"You don't look too bad yourself," I lied. He looked gorgeous in a simple pair of blue khakis and a dark purple golf shirt. His shirt set off his eyes, and I stood there a full minute, feeling warm and gooey inside. I grab my left hand before I hit myself. "Where are we going?"

"I know this place," he said, "with great food, great martinis, and a wonderful atmosphere. But now I see how beautiful you look, I'm not sure if it's the right place."

I wait for him to continue. When he didn't say anything, I shrug my shoulders, "Dude, you pick, and you pay."

Zack laughed. "No problem. I always pay on my dates." Oh my gosh, I thought. We were on our second date.

We head out to a different car, a black BMW 320i. Zack holds open the door for me, then I watched as he walks in front. He waved to someone across the lot. So far, this had the potential to be a good evening.

Zack turned the radio to a Red Sox game. I can't remember who they are playing. Ric would know. He is probably watching it on TV with my dad. That is if they have a TV. He hadn't been gone a day, and I already worried about him.

"Do you think you can clear up this mess in less than two weeks?" I asked.

Zack held my hand in his, resting his left on the steering wheel, and squeezed gently. "I sure hope so," he said. "I think we have most of the puzzle pieces. We just need to get them in order, catch the bad guys, and then you can put your life back together."

It sounds so easy when he said it. "Will I be able to put my life back to the way it was?" His hand feels good, reliable, safe, holding mine.

"Maxi, no one can put their lives back exactly the way it was when something of this magnitude happens. One can only hope and pray when everything settles, it's better than before."

I nod in agreement and tell myself it couldn't get any worst. Of course, when it is all put back together, will there be us? My free hand hit the side of my head. Zack raises his eyebrow in my direction.

"I deserved that," I told him. "Trust me on this one. So who's up to bat?"

"I think they're near the top of the order, you know, Crisp, Papi, Manny."

"I wouldn't know. That's Ric's department. I watch the games with an expert."

We drove down Rte 154 out of town, along the Connecticut River, catching glances of the lights from the bows of boats moving slow. The radio filled the void of silence in the background. Zack turned onto 148 in Chester and headed inland. The quaint colonial downtown area of galleries, bistros, and specialty shops

178

move quickly passed. He took a left at a faintly lit sign. He had chosen Sages. I love Sages. How did he know?

"So, what do you think?" he asked, backing into an open parking space by the entrance. Zack must be the luckiest parker on earth. In season he'd be lucky to find a space in the lot across the street, never mind across from the entrance.

"I love this place! How did you know?"

He grabbed my hand to help me out of the car. We stroll over the covered bridge towards the main doors that lead to the tavern.

"Lucky guess," he answered. I could see by the sparkles in his eyes he is pretty darn pleased with himself.

"Freakin', Pete?"

"That too." It still amazed me how my brother is in contact with everyone except me. How messed up is that? "Hi, we have a reservation under Brady for two."

The hostess beamed at Zack. I'd say she is in her late twenties and dressed to the nines in a long maroon cocktail gown with a slit up the side to show off her perfectly sculpted legs. She must work out to keep that body in shape. Adding to the illusion were five-inch heels, not that she needed to be taller. She towered over Zack.

Taking his arm, she led him around the podium. "Right this way, Mr. Brady."

Zack still had my hand in his. He gave it a quick squeeze. I am happy I am not PMSing because the wench would have broken fingers. I bet her boobs are fake. They are so perky; they must have come out of a box.

I smile up at him. He must get this all the time. How could an average person like me compete with the hotties who would always be chasing him? It would be Jon all over again, not that Jon was as good looking as Zack. No matter, it is the same with all men.

He had said he'd be done in a few weeks. I supposed that once he is done, I'd be done too. Man, it isn't fair for the same guy to break your heart twice in the same lifetime. There should be a once-per-life rule. You'd get to team up again during reincarnation for additional cracks. You know – ok, so you broke her heart last lifetime. Now when you two are sent back, it is her turn type deal.

Not only is this unfair, but I thought Pete had probably set us up. Freakin' Pete. Why didn't he mind his own business or at least do his deeds in person instead of long-distance?

"Maxi, is this okay?" Zack stood by a table that overlooked the water outside a large window. Now that I am paying attention, I could hear the gurgle of the tributary that ran under the restaurant. That may be how the restaurant gets some of its electric power.

"Yeah, fine," I answer, snapping myself back to reality. I looked around. The table for two is lit by a single candle, and light came in from the window. The place itself is rustic, with exposed beams of weathered wood. Minimal decorations hung on the wood exposed walls. Fresh wildflowers graced our table.

I'd only eaten in the bar at Sages, so this all is a new sensory experience. The bar is very dark, with no windows, and still smelled like cigarettes, even though no one had smoked in there for years. It had a beautiful stone fireplace as its center. Comfortable couches and chairs with high backs are scattered around in clusters.

The restaurant part is different. In the bar, the space is open. Here, upstairs in the dining room, we were secluded. Is this a good thing? I guess, like everything else, I have to wait and see.

"I would like a Stoli's martini straight up with olives. And you, Max?" Zack directed the waitress's attention to me. I hadn't been listening.

"Oh, I'll have the same." I wave my hand in the air as if we order drinks together routinely. Zack raised his eyebrow but said nothing. He pulled my chair out for me. This is very nice yet very awkward at the same time. I sat and leaned forward, resting my chin in my hands.

Instead of sitting across from me, like the table is set up, Zack rearranged the flowers, candle, salt, and pepper shakers to the side and moved his chair next to mine. My head tilted over onto my right hand, and I put on a dreamy smile. Zack had his arm on the back of my chair. I could feel electric jolts from his light touch on the back of my shoulder. He grinned. Maybe this all wouldn't turn out that bad.

"Here are your drinks," the hostess purred. "Well,, look at you two, all cozy." Zack reached up to remove the glasses from her tray, probably thinking, as I did, she might spill on me.

"Thanks," he said dismissively with a charming smile. The waitress walked away silently. "I thought we might be taking a bath there."

"Yeah, it looked like those drinks might be heading for me," I replied. "Thanks for saving me." I blatantly flirt. What the hell, right?

"To life getting better than normal," Zack toasted raising his glass.

"I'll drink to that," I gently touch my glass to his. I tried to be careful because as much as I liked drinking from martini glasses, I didn't do it often. Alcohol and I don't mix. I did think a good buzz, minus the hangover, of course, might help me forget my kid is away in government protection. There is more I need to forget, too.

I pick out my olives to savor the sour taste of each one. In my younger days, I would ask for a glass of olives with a martini on the side. This one is the opposite, although the three olives on the stick were all jumbo-sized. I hope they help soak up alcohol as lightweight Maxi is already buzzed on two sips. Wheeee!

"So, Max, what were you thinking of to eat?" Zack had his menu open.

"I don't know." I sat up straight and stared at the leather-bound piece of paper. The combination of Stoli's buzz and lack of light made it difficult to read. I guess I could do what I usually did and order the same. Then again, that's how I got the martini. "We should wait for the specials. We seem to do better with those."

"Yes, we do." Zack leaned over to kiss me on the cheek, lingering close. "Yes, we do," he repeated in a softer voice. I imagined the space where his lips touched me glow in a pale blue haze.

"Yeah." I couldn't think of anything else. I am balmy, buzzed, and sitting in a romantic restaurant with Zack Brady for the second time in my life. If I died that night, it would be okay. My left hand slapped the side of my head. What am I thinking? Ric needed me! Man, I hoped Ric is alright.

"Ric is fine," Zack said as if he read my mind.

"How did you know?"

He pulled out a cell phone, scrolled through his contacts, and hit send. "See for yourself," he said as he handed it over to me.

Seconds later, Ric's voice came through. "Hello."

"Hey, dude. What's happening?" My shoulders sank downward in relief. My baby was okay!

"Mom! You should see this place! It is so cool. It's got a lake, a pool, pool tables, Nintendo, awesome food, and guess what?"

"What?"

"They know Uncle Pete! Can you believe it?"

Of course, they did. "No, I can't," Freakin' Pete is quickly replacing my old motto, Jon Sucks. "Are Gram and Pops having fun too?"

"Pops is playing cards with a couple old guys like him, and Gram and I are going to shoot pool with some of the kids. There are even kids my age here. Mom, this place is so sweet."

"Tell her we are having a blast and not to worry," my mom shouted in the background.

"Hey, Mom, I gotta go," Ric said, obviously distracted by something. "I love you."

"I love you too, dude. Hugs and kisses all around."

"You got it!" The phone went silent. I pushed end and handed it back to Zack.

"Thank you," I say in a voice above a whisper.

"Anytime." He moved over and pressed his soft lips against mine. The blue electric haze circled around my face.

"Are you ready to order?" the waitress interrupts my wow moment.

Zack smiled up at her, and her stiff body softened. Do you suppose he has that effect on every woman on earth? "Could you tell us the specials, please?"

The waitress beamed. "No problem. We have a roasted beet salad with oranges and goat cheese appetizer, along with a cold carrot almond soup." Yes to the salad; nose wrinkle to the carrot soup. "For entrees we have organic pan-fried salmon served over barley pilaf with grilled zucchini and yellow squash, slow-roasted chicken with our own barbeque sauce served with potato salad and corn, and filet mignon marinated in light Italian seasonings served with fresh grilled green beans and garlic mashed potatoes." She took a deep breath and gave us both a genuine smile.

"May I?" Zack asked. I nod to go ahead. "Okay, because my date has weird tastes in food…"

"Hey, I represent that remark."

"Continuing on," he waves me off, "we would like the beet salad, the salmon, and the filet. Is that okay with you, Max?"

"Perfect."

The server disappeared. I looked down at my martini glass. Somehow it got emptied. How did that happen? The server reappeared and silently filled it, leaving the silver decanter sitting on the table near Zack.

"Can I please have more olives?" I asked as she walked away. I need a stomach coating quickly. I downed one without even remembering it. I could usually handle one, or one and a half, but any more and Zack is going to have a wild woman on his hands who wouldn't remember a thing in the morning. Probably not a good thing since we were only on our second date, we were staying at the same place, and I still thought when everything got settled there is potential for a third.

"I shouldn't drink this," I fiddled with my glass.

"Then don't."

I took a long sip and savored the burn of the vodka on the back of my throat. This is so good, I told myself.

The server returned with a basket of warm bread along with a tray of various spreads arranged carefully on a silver tray. I should eat some of that. The bread would soak up my drink better than the olives had.

"I'm glad you and I caught up," I heard Zack say.

"Me too," I murmur. The funny thing about me getting a buzz is I become incapable of having a conversation. Everything that came out of my mouth sounded like blah, blah, blah, blah to me. So, I made an effort to sit and be quiet without falling asleep. When I have to talk, I hope what I have to say would make sense.

I helped myself to a piece of brown bread from the basket, immediately tearing off little pieces to put in my mouth. My other hand grabbed the glass of ice water. I take a long gulp. My body requested to eat and drink something alcohol-free.

Zack took my left hand in his. We both stared at the hypnotic running water of the stream. I wish we could stay like this. I should have learned long ago drinking was not my thing. Way back in my twenties, I got so lit on a date I spent most of the evening in the Ladies room trying to convince myself I wasn't drunk. I got some bizarre looks from women who entered to see me talking to myself in the mirror. The guy I was with turned out to be a real jerk, and I was his flavor of the month.

"So, Maxi," Zack tried to start a conversation, "I take it you're not much of a drinker anymore?"

I could feel my face turn bright red. I am grateful for the candlelight.

"I've never been all that good with alcohol. But I do love a good martini." I lift my glass to toast him. Zack gently removes it from my hand. He places it across the table just as the waitress brings out the beet salad.

"Is there a problem with the drink?"

"No problem. We only wanted one drink. I think we're good." He hands her the glass and the decanter, then shifts his glass in her direction. After she gathered it all up, Zack held up one finger for her to wait a minute. "I would like a ginger ale. How about you, Max?"

"I'm good with water." I toast him. He is too smooth. I fiddle with my napkin. "Thanks."

"No problem. I know you think of me as this big party dude, but to tell you the truth, Max, I'm more into beer on weekends and water during the week. I figure the ginger ale will take the buzz off the martini for me, you know?"

"That's cool. There are times when I want to go out and get smashed," I admit.

"Like the old days." He sips his water while watching me over his glass.

"Yeah, like the old days, but the new Maxi can't handle the next day. I can drink a little wine now and then but only every once in a while."

"I know what you mean." We went back to staring out the window. I reach over with my fork to scoop a few tiny beets with goat cheese, then popped it into my mouth. Sweet and tart and orange and- "Wow, this is amazing."

Zack tasted it too and gestured in agreement. After that, we didn't talk because we were both working our way to the middle of the plate.

"I wonder what the extra spice is. I can't put my finger on it." I put more salad in my mouth.

"Tarragon," Zack answered with authority.

"How can you tell?" It amazed me he would recognize such an obscure spice.

"The sweetness. It just sticks out." Zack put the last bite onto his fork and extended it over to me. "It's all yours, Max." I lean over to gently take his fork in my mouth. Yum.

"So, Zack, I have an essential question to ask you."

"This sounds serious, Max. Yes, I will be yours tonight if you'll have me."

Jolts of heat flew back at me, and I fall into silence. Trying to recoup, I say, "No, that's not it. The question is…" I pause for effect, "Do you like Indian food?"

"That is a serious question, and the answer is yes." He is mocking me while I have hot flashes. I told myself after being married to Jon, I will not compromise anywhere in my life again, and what happened? I had this guy in front of me who so far had answered every question correctly. It is like he had known me forever.

"Awesome, because I know this great place."

The waitress showed up with our entrees and placed them in the middle of the table. She then produced two extra plates.

"You two look like the surf and turf types," she smiled.

"Dig in," Zack gestured. We ate in silence, enjoying the savory mashed potatoes and lightly spiced filet. The green beans burst with flavor and were still slightly crisp to the taste. Somehow the beans cooked perfect, yet the squash overcooked. Neither of us ate more than one mouthful of barley. With garlic mashed potatoes that good, why bother.

"It's so nice to eat with someone who actually eats," Zack wiped his mouth on his napkin. "Have you ever gone to dinner with someone who orders and then picks at their food? That drives me up a wall."

"I used to do that," I confess. "When I was younger, I would be embarrassed to eat in front of people. I got over it." I gesture towards my stomach.

"I'm glad," Zack replied, "and for the record, your body is great. I almost fell in your parents' pool that first day."

"Oh, really?" Now it is my turn to raise an eyebrow.

"Max, if I saw you on the street, I'd think you were twenty-something." He caught my smile and added, "You know you look good."

"You don't look so bad yourself." It's a good line, so I tend to overuse it. The martini buzz remained enough to keep me confident. This time I lean over to kiss Zack. I could taste a little beet, along with garlic mashed potatoes. The blue stars swirled all over me again. Zack broke the kiss and sat back.

"What am I going to do with you?" We were wearing goofy smiles, looking at each other, and not saying a word.

"Do you two want dessert?" the waitress appeared at our table, again, "I know, check please." She walked away, and we both started to laugh. Zack kissed me again. I loved the feel of his lips on mine. They gave off little electric surprises that were delicious.

Zack paid the bill, and we walked out to the main lobby hand in hand.

"Wait here a minute," he said as he headed over to the men's room. A few minutes later, he comes back, and we headed out. The hostess called after us to have a lovely evening.

Chapter Twenty-One

Zach took a left out of the parking lot then headed south on route nine, taking the more direct way back. He drove in silence. I observed his eyes glancing back and forth between the rear-view mirror and the road. I look at the speedometer to see he is doing about eighty. I thought about warning him about the speed traps that were notorious along this route. Then again, why bother? He probably knew all the cops.

Did you ever have one of those moments when your body tells you to be scared, but your brain isn't getting the hint? Well,, my nauseous pit is in full action as my cell phone started to ring. At the same time I bent over to search for my phone in my purse, Zack said, "Oh crap!" and sped up.

"Maxi, I need to talk to you. It's an emergency." Jon's whiney voice came through the static.

"Talk to my lawyer," I said as I started to hang up. Jon is still babbling, but I am only catching every other word.

"Maxi, Zach, and Gert…" He got my attention now. Those were two names I never wanted to hear with an 'and' in the middle! I listen more carefully.

"I can't hear you." The call is breaking up too much, and I had to hit end. Then remembering to whom I was speaking, I shrugged my shoulders. "If it's

190

important, he'll call back, right?" I am curious why he would mention Zach and Gert in the same sentence, but I tossed my phone back into my purse.

There is a big white pickup truck pulling alongside us. Zack hit the brake at the same time something big smashed against our rear window, causing it to crack but not shatter.

"What the….?" I exclaimed.

"Maxi, stay down," Zack yelled as he pushed my head below the dash. I struggle to fight him, but he is too strong. As he let up, my body banged against the door. He swung the car around, and I look up to see us flying down the exit four ramp. In a panic, I looked back in time to catch the white truck making a U-turn in the middle of the highway.

"Crap, he's coming back," I scream.

Zack's eyes squinted. His jaw tightened. My dinner started to make its way back up as I watched him drive with one hand on his cell and the other on the wheel. He turned south on Route 154, took a quick right onto one of the side roads, and then cut the lights. The only sound in the car is the heavy sound of our breathing. We waited. My nausea began to settle, yet I couldn't control my shuttering body.

"Zack?"

He put his hand up to shush me. After what appeared to be an eternity, he took out his cell.

"Those sons of a… How dare they?" Zack punched in numbers, each with an exclamation of words. "I can't believe they've gone this far! I'll, I'll…"

He inhaled a deep breath. "Someone just shot at me," he said into the phone. His voice was far calmer than the vibrations off his twitching body. He listened while glaring out at the road. "Yeah, it held." I heard excitement coming through his earpiece. It actually sounded like someone rejoicing. "I don't think the fact your bulletproof windows held together is a reason to celebrate me getting shot at." The comment came with a tired smile.

At least I am holding up Well,. I hadn't puked or soiled myself. And it's not every day I get shot at, or for that matter, my house gets broken into, or put my kid in protective custody.

And here come the tears. What tough gal cries this much?

"What time did that happen?" I heard him say. Great, we have more bad news. I am already a sniveling mess. Wait, one more thing? As long as it is not…

"Is it Ric?" I whisper. He shakes his head, no. I sat silently, praying he'd share whatever is going on no matter how bad it is. Please, God, don't let anything happen to anyone close to me. I had enough excitement for one lifetime.

"She's here with me, so I'll let her know. Thanks." Zack hung up the phone, leaned his head back against his headrest, and took in a deep breath. "We were having a good time tonight before all this, right?"

"I thought so."

"Good. Me too. I needed to know because now I need to ruin it." I wait. Zack twisted his body towards mine. "Maxi, who called you back on the highway?"

I flashback to Jon's voice and the garbled sound of Gert and Zack's name coming through. "It was Jon, babbling about something."

Zack shook his head. "Okay, question number two. I need you to think, Maxi. Was there anything of value aboard your boat?"

"I told you before. No. There is a safe on board, but it has been emptied. I cleaned it out after the repair guys Jon sent broke in. Gert had advised me to get the contents off the boat, and I actually listened to her. Why?" This sounded serious. I could tell because the car is quiet while he took his time answering. Zack chose his words carefully.

"Gert told you to clean out the safe?" I nodded. "Did she know you did it?"

I motion with my hand towards the door, "I don't know. Maybe, she did then again, maybe not. I haven't shared a lot with Gert lately, just business stuff."

"Why is that?"

Good question, Zack. "I'm not sure. It's one of those should I or shouldn't I things. Plus, I've been so busy getting shot at and broken into I haven't had a chance." Sarcasm is the lowest form of humor and one of the things I resorted to when I got scared or nervous. I knew what I was saying wasn't funny, but what the heck, it made Zack laugh.

"You are cute, Maxi. Very cute. But back to business. Was the boat up for sale?"

"I had to try to sell it to give half the proceeds to Jon. Gert said if I did it this way, it would speed up the divorce."

"Good old Gert." Zack shook his head again, ran his hands through his hair, and returned his gaze on me. I felt naked, but not in a good way. "Maxi was the boat for sale?" he repeated.

He is far too dangerous. "Yes." Zack grinned.

"I have some good news and some bad news. Which do you want first?"

Headlights came from the main road flashed across the street entrance, sending shivers up my spine. The shadow that passed resembled a sedan. Thank heavens it wasn't a truck. I might have wet myself.

"I'll take good news." I needed good news.

"Optimist, I like that." Zack leaned over to kiss me on my cheek. The sparks were still there, yet I am thinking this guy's timing is way off. "Maxi, you don't need to sell your boat," he announced, using a fake used car salesman smile.

"You mean I can keep her?" This is good news. Nice to know something is going my way since someone had just shot at me a few minutes ago. I could still keep my sanctuary. Yeah!

"No," Zack answered in the same voice. I knew it appeared too good to be true. "But you can collect insurance money." He sounded like one of those game show guys.

"Did someone steal her?" If so, that is one stupid boat thief. Why would anyone take the Slug Puppy when there is a brand new sleek, gorgeous vessel in the slip next her worth quadruple my baby's worth? The worth being monetary, of course, not emotional. The people next to me obviously had no taste in boats.

"Yes." Zack nods. "And they blew her up in the middle of the sound around nine this evening. Oh, this is the bad news." Zack hit the side of his head. He looked over at me, and his smile faded. His whole face is a series of wrinkles. "Maxi, are you okay?"

I couldn't speak, so I did the next easiest thing; I opened up the car door, stuck my head out, and puked up my dinner. Then after wiping my mouth, I erupted in tears. "Why would anyone want to blow up a perfectly good boat?" I wailed. I sounded like a spoiled debutante, something I had never been nor would ever be. This isn't turning into the evening I had thought.

Zack handed me a piece of gum then put his arms around me while I wept into his chest. His hands moved lightly around my back, giving me a slice of peace.

Who on earth would want to blow up my boat? It was such a beautiful vessel. I had such wonderful memories of playing hokey on it and floating off Duck Island away from the stress of running a business or having my husband leave me. I remembered picking her out from a catalog at the boat dealers and Ric coming up with the name Slug Puppy, a tribute to our last dopey Labrador. We had an unveiling when the sign company finally finished putting the name across the back. My parents bought us round life preservers, as a happy sailing gift. The more memories that flashed into my head, the more tears I shed on Zack's shirt.

"Why?" I hit Zack with one fist.

"Ouch," he said, rubbing his arm. I peered up at him, then placed my head back down. He kissed the top of my head, still rubbing my back tenderly.

I thought of all the people who didn't like my boat. The people with the slip next to mine who always thought I was going to dent their new boat when I docked? Nope, couldn't be them. They'd go after my insurance company. They had already threatened to put in a claim against me many times while they sat on their bow watching me try to back in instead of getting up to help me.

Then there was Jon. He wanted me to give up the boat when we first split up, and he always complained about our sharing agreement. Like a little whining baby, he kept complaining to the court I took the boat out on his days. Heh, heh, heh. I guess that was true sometimes. He is so stupid, though. He'd get less money by blowing it up because, without the asset, we'd get paid on current value, not replacement value. That is the way he set up our boat insurance. And if he is that stupid, he deserved to get royally screwed by the insurance company.

I laughed aloud. Zack put his worried look on again. I shook him off while trying to think of more suspects. Gert always hated the boat, but it couldn't be Gert. She is still my lawyer after all, and truth be told, despite everything, Gert is still my friend.

Who else would want to do this? "It has to be Jon," I said. "It has to be. He's so stupid he probably thought he'd get more money this way or at least get his share faster." I reach onto the floor for my purse. "I need to call Gert."

Promptly Zack knocked the phone out of my hand. "No, Gert." He had done this before. I had a flashback to when my house got broken into. He had used the same tone of voice. Come to think of it, Pete had Gert issues too. I bet Pete slammed Gert to Zack, and that is why he is doing the "No Gert" gig. Freakin', Pete strikes again!

"Gert is my legal counsel, along with my friend. Shouldn't she--?"

196

Zack's hand went up. He reached for his key and started the car.

"No, Gert, Maxi." Without headlights, he pulled out on the road, staying on the back roads to get back to town. "I need to get you back to the condo."

I opted to take another approach. "Who was shooting at us?"

"I don't know." His hands gripped the wheel so tightly they'd probably leave imprints.

"Zack, I need more than that," I started to control my voice the best I could. "Hey! This is my life! I don't know what's going on or why. I mean, come on." I am on a roll now. My hands were flying around Italian style. "Zack, I have had my house broken in to, my office ransacked, my boat invaded and now blown up. My brother isn't calling me back, but he's called everyone around me. I wouldn't be surprised to hear Ric hung out with his Uncle Pete in New Hampshire." I turn my body to touch his arm. It stiffened on contact. "Zack, I need to know more!" Tears dripped down my face.

Zack peeked over at me and shook his head. He drove in silence. We followed back roads through Essex into Mayberry in complete silence. As we got closer to the condo, he picked up his phone and said, "Bert" into the speaker.

"Is it safe to come back?" Bert must be talking because Zack had gone silent. His jawline had become more prominent, and the thinking lines across his nose returned. "Fine." He threw his phone on the floor by my feet.

"Maxi, I promise I will explain as much as I can to you, but I need you to do me a big favor." I nod, "I need you to go straight into the condo when we get back. I will park and join you quickly. Please go in and shut the door and wait for me. And Max," he scrutinized me now, "please, just do this." Zack had that pained expression that only the fathers of daughters get. The one that says I know you can smile and con me out of this, but please, just this once, surprise me and listen. I knew the look well because, at times, my dad had sported it too.

"Okay." Talk about your blind faith. I hope my gut is working correctly this evening. The first thing I planned to do after that door closed is to try to get in touch with Pete. With my luck, I'd be leaving yet another message. You've got to love your siblings.

Chapter Twenty-Two

I do as instructed, one hand in my purse rummaging for my phone. I have all intentions of swearing at my brother's voice mail. As I opened the door, I hear voices in the living room.

I bit my bottom lip as I shuffle on the tiled floor. My stomach decided now is a good time for more flip flops. I needed to make a move.

My gut instructed me to run outside and meet Zack. My horoscope said Something about an exciting evening that wouldn't lead to romance but could in the future. All systems were directing me to get the heck out.

What did I do?

"Hello? Who's there?" I call out as I walk towards the voices.

"We're in here," I hear a female voice. I come around the corner to stop short in the doorway. A stunning blonde sat on in the middle of the sofa. She should be on a fashion runway, not here in my living room with a gun strapped across her blouse. Next to her sat another guy who also looked familiar. He might have been at the boat dock with the Westbrook police, but I was not sure. Stress did that to me sometimes. I got what my grandmother called CRS syndrome.

"Hi, you must be Maxi." The blonde moved towards me with the grace of a dancer. Her hand was outstretched. I shook it and tried to smile. "I'm Bert. I work with Zack. It's so nice to finally meet you."

"Nice to meet you too," I force out. Bert from the car conversation is a woman. And she's a gorgeous woman too. As I noted at Sage's, I am entirely out of my league.

"This is Al. He works with us too." She gestured towards the person standing by the window.

"Hey." Al waved at me.

"Hey, back at you," I said. Bert took me by the elbow and led me back to the couch. She sank down into the cushions and patted the pillow next to her, inviting me to sit. I followed her lead to sit on the opposite side, leaning back against the armrest. I crossed my legs and my arms. One foot unconsciously made a little shaking movement.

"So, how was dinner?" Bert asked, adding, "I hear Sages is excellent."

"Yeah, it's one of my favorites," I said. "The food is good, and the place is very laid back." I shook while she sat there looking completely relaxed. I considered taking deep breaths, but I didn't want to start hyperventilating. "I've always eaten at the bar, so being in the restaurant was a treat." Bert sported a serene look on her face. "They make excellent martinis too." I didn't want her to concentrate on me because she could be a mind reader. You know one of those special agents you hear about with psychic abilities. Where the heck is Zach?

"I haven't been there in years," Bert broke the stillness. "Do they still make good desserts?"

I check out her body. Unless she is a member of the Lucky Gene Club, this woman did not eat dessert. "They do, but we were too full." Zack's voice echoed outside the front door. I couldn't figure out the conversation, but it sounded like a one-sided argument.

"We didn't agree to this. You know, and I know something changed in the way these guys do business. I need to get her out of here now!" Zack slammed through the door, stopping short as I watch his eyes meet Bert's. "I'll be there in an hour," he pressed end. Zack leaned over to give Bert a kiss on her porcelain cheek. "When did you get here?" he asked.

"About five minutes before Maxi." They watched at each other the way lovers or keepers of a secret do. I am paranoid, but then I am totally an outsider here. I wanted to run away from the car wreck I am watching because this car wreck is my life.

Zack sat between us, casually resting his hand on my knee. The rest of his body angled towards Bert. He slowly rubbed his thumb along the side of my leg. I watched Bert's eyes take this in.

"So, who were you screaming at?" she asked, brushing her hair back casually with one hand.

"Sal." They both start to laugh like Sal was a private joke.

"Sal is our boss," Bert explained, nodding her head in my direction. I gave her the chin nod back.

"Yeah," added Zack. "He is our boss and keeper." They started cackling again, sounding like a couple of teenagers. I didn't like it. I wondered where Al disappeared to. Maybe he is out back grabbing a smoke?

"Did Sal give you instructions?"

Zack washed his free hand over his face. "I need to go to New Haven and conduct a conversation with him in person." I jumped. Zack gave my knee a quick squeeze. "Maxi, you're going to need to hang out here a while…"

"Dude, I was shot at tonight!" I remind him.

"Yeah, they found the vehicle. I need to go to New Haven and ID it. I'm leaving you in capable hands." His hand flew up in the air making the silence move.

"Don't you hate when he does that?" Bert said.

"Very much so." I crossed my arms as my right foot began to tap. This was not a good sign for Zack.

"He has been doing that talk to the hand thing for years. Drives us all crazy, right, Zack?" Bert directed the comment towards me, yet I knew she meant it for Zack. My little voice screamed that there is a lot of history here.

"Hello, I'm here," Zack waved. "Maxi, you're not in any danger. It's going to be okay. Al's here. I need to leave for a little while."

I watch his face, "Zack, is Ric really someplace safe, and am I really going to be okay? Why can't I come with you?"

Zack hesitated, glanced at Bert, who looked back with *you're on your own* expression, and then calmly replied, "You're okay. Ric's okay. And you can't come because you're safer here." He marched out of the room.

"Well, that clarifies everything," I threw my hands up in the air. Bert stood and moved about, gathering her purse, car keys, and jacket off the adjacent chair.

"Maxi, it was a pleasure meeting you," she said, shaking my hand.

I watched her follow Zack, and I heard quiet voices coming from the hall. The front door opened and closed, which is usually a welcome sound, providing the right person stepped through it.

"Hey, Maxi," I heard Zack call, "can you come here for a minute?"

I creep into the hallway to track his voice. He sat in a high back leather executive chair behind a desk in the side room.

"Hey, you." He reached over, took my hand, then pulled me towards him. "I guess I have some explaining to do."

I indicated yes with my free hand. "She wants you," I add as I sit on top of his thighs, leaning into his chest.

"Bert?"

"No, Al. Who'd ya think, Zack?" His legs are all muscle, yet I couldn't get my butt comfortable sitting on top of him like this. I wanted to be close, yet I didn't want him to feel the pain on my boney butt.

"I hoped it was you." That comment rushed through me. "Anyway," Zack let me off the hook on that one, "I owe you an explanation. I know that. Unfortunately, I do need to ID the vehicle, and it's impounded in New Haven at the Connecticut headquarters so…"

"You have to leave." How convenient that both Zack and Bert had to leave at the same time. I need to stay put as crazy people break into my spaces and take target practice using me as the bull's eye. I guessed it is his time to move on because his next conquest is waiting in the wing. "Great." I decided at this point, watching the floor is much better than looking at him.

"No, it's not great. But I need to, and I will be right back. I promise. Call your mom. Talk to Ric. Watch TV. You need to sit tight. Al will be around if you need anything." Zack reached out to stroke my cheek. I closed my eyes and imagined he was leaving blue streaks all down my face. Later my tears would wash them away.

I open my eyes to look into his soft brown eyes. They move back and forth between my gaze and my lips leaving little tingles along the way. He lifts my chin to touch my lips to his. I tighten my grip around his neck and bring him closer. His tongue flirts with mine while beautiful blue stars exploded in my eyes. I let out a quiet sigh as his finger brushed over my left breast. Even though my dress and bra, his touch ignited a desire within me.

My mixed feelings began to surface as Bert's face popped in among the stars. He is still moving his lips on mine, yet my imagination had moved on to him and Bert walking off into the sunset together while I sat in the car.

Zack broke away then sat holding on to me tight. I could feel his chest pounding and the warmth of his ragged breath on my neck. "It's going to be alright," he told me. "I'm going to take care of this, and we're going to be alright."

Zack walked out the door. I went into the bedroom, laid down across the bed, and stared at the ceiling. I am not sure when or how I fell asleep, but when I looked out the door, a bright light came streaming in. It could only be sunshine. I had survived the night.

I stretched out my body, wondered why Zack hadn't returned, and what is left in the refrigerator for breakfast. We didn't have any leftovers from the night before, so someone is going to need to go get food. My guess is that someone is Al because I am on lockdown.

Chapter Twenty-Three

I've said it before, and I'll say it again. I am not very good at following directions. I like to be the boss. That is why I had to stop working for Bob Carlson, I wanted to be in charge too much, and in the corporate media world, I always had someone above me who interpreted my moves as crushing their toes.

This could be why Zack had one of his minions sitting across the parking lot in a white van watching the condo. I could see him sitting over there, eating a sandwich as he rotated his attention between my door and the marina. I didn't recognize the guy, and I wondered where Al had gone. I thought he went out to get some breakfast for us, but he had left over an hour ago, and he hadn't returned.

Having this big guy I didn't know, in a van, sitting in my parking lot, did not make me feel more secure. It kind of freaked me out.

The last thing Zack had said before he took off the night before, "Stay inside the condo. Listen to me this time. Do not leave, Max. Not even for a stress-reducing walk to the point. I mean it."

I guess he didn't trust me to listen. I don't know if I'd trust me to listen either. I did know I would feel much better if Zack stayed next to me instead of taking off to do God knows what. It would be good to feel his arms around me this morning. He might be used to getting shot at, but it is a whole new universe for me.

The only thing I want to know is why. "WHY?" I scream. I stand up to pace. Walking sometimes helped me think. I needed to figure this all out. Who could I have pissed off so much they'd take a shot at me? I didn't think Jon was that mad. I didn't have any enemies, at least none I knew of. I started going up and down the stairs stopping to ponder. No one came to mind, not even my sister-in-law, who I know is crazy but not psycho. Then there is Jon, but he is not really an enemy. He is more of a lost alliance. There is a difference.

I thought the movement would calm me down. My mind is going a mile a minute. Bursts of exercise did not do the trick. "Crap!" Add swearing to the list of things not working either. I could watch TV. Now there is a waste of mind and time. I found the remote, turned on the television, and proceeded to go through each channel. News, news, sitcom, shopping, sports, sitcom, movie, news, news, Oprah, soap, Springer, movie, nothing. I hit the off switch, walked back upstairs, and continued to stare out the window. It is another perfect beach day with lots of sun and from what I could see very little wind. It would be a great day to go out on a boat if I still owned one.

I had to wonder what kind of person would blow up a perfectly good boat. The Slug Puppy was a beautiful vessel. Some guy had brought over the pieces the Coast Guard had been able to recover, and a few parts are sitting downstairs on the living room floor. When I had looked at the burnt life ring, I finally saw a reason to get out of Mayberry. I mean, come on, they went through all the trouble to steal my beautiful, old boat, and then they took it out in the sound and blew it to pieces. Why? For kicks? There was nothing of value on board. This went way beyond your everyday run of the mill crook or wise-ass high school kid.

Zack had tried to convince me it all is random, and one situation had nothing to do with the other stuff, yet I don't believe him. Someone hated me. Someone hated me besides Jon and the Tart. I had some mystery psychopath on my hands.

I couldn't believe Jon would resort to this type of violence. I mean, he still is a hippy at heart—a slimy, disgusting sleaze bag scammer but a hippy nonetheless. Just thinking of him aggravated the hell out of me. I wanted to know how he found out about my business deal with Bob Carlson. Another lovely message left on my voice mail. "Max, he wants half the gross business sale proceeds, including a percentage of your consultant fee." Gert got straight into it, and then told me to call her back ASAP! How had Jon ever gotten the balls to go for the sale proceeds in court plus alimony? This is so beyond me. Whatever happened to male pride? I am supposed to be divorced by now with all this shit behind me. The judge had been all set for us sign papers, but then Jon had to go and get greedy. I had no idea what is going on there because I was instructed not to call Gert.

Thank heavens Gert would take care of everything in the divorce department. With all the other stuff happening, I am fortunate she is staying on top of the divorce thing, at least I thought she is. All I should need had to do is sign papers, speaking of which, there were a bunch of them at my office. Those papers

208

marked the end of mine and Jon's marriage. I could only hope that chapter would finally be over. If I had known it would be this easy to get full custody of Ric, I'd give up the business months ago. I am happy to do it, but I am not willing to pay Jon alimony too. The next time we went to court, I hoped the judge would see Jon was all about the money, and I am about being a responsible parent.

My cell phone is plugged in by the table, and although I didn't want to get into all of this with her, I dialed my mom and pressed send. She'd had Ric for twenty-four hours, someplace in New Hampshire Zack had suggested.

Just hearing Mom's voice would let me know everything is going to be ok. Gosh, sometimes I resorted back to a little kid calling her mommy to make me feel better, safer. And I wanted to know if she heard from my jerk face brother Pete lately.

"Hello." Her raspy voice came through the line.

"Hey, Mom, how's it going?" I sank into one of the chairs upstairs and watched the clouds float by the bay window.

"Maxi, is that you? Is everything ok?" That is my mom - always, Miss Positive. One thing about my mom that is so creepy, she always knows when something is up, even if I didn't tell her. I used to think one of my brothers ratted me out, but now I wonder.

"Yes and no. How about you? How's Ric doing?" If I change the subject, I wouldn't worry her.

"Ric's fine. He's at the lake with your father. This place is nice, nothing fancy, you know. Just a few cabins along a lake. It's been pretty relaxing. They've got a great restaurant." I exhale a sigh of relief. Ric was okay. My parents were okay. This is good.

"That sounds great. Nice and mellow. I could use that." It is definitely preferable to getting shot at and having strange men keeping me prisoner in a condo.

"We've been having a wonderful time. I think we're coming back early. I heard something about a couple days. Besides, Ric misses you." That thought torched my heart. At least I had one male in my life who still loved me.

"Great. Let me know what time. I'll try to come and pick him up." If I am released from my prison, I thought. I hadn't felt alone until then. I needed my kid and my goofy family around me. Things were getting too hairy to be by myself. At that point, I would even consider Jon a port in the storm.

My hand hit the side of my head. What am I thinking? That is being desperate!

"Maxi, are you still there? You are breaking up…"

"Yeah, I'm here, Mom. Thanks for all your help with everything."

"Maxi, Maxi, Maxi, you don't always have to be the brave one, you know."

"Yeah, I know." Oh boy. That did it. Now I wanted to cry but didn't want my Mom to worry, so I cut the call short. "I'll talk to you tomorrow. Give Ric a hug and kiss for me."

"Will do. Love you, Max." And with that, she disconnected. I wept like a baby.

I sat Indian style on the carpet, crossed my arms, and scrunched my face up. And to top it off, Zack left me all alone to do nothing but think and sulk and just just…. Crap, the tears started dripping again. I had not cried this much since…ever. I am definitely losing what little is left of my mind. During my fit, bells start ringing in the distance.

"Damn," I exclaimed as I reach for my cell phone.

"Hello," I choked into the receiver.

"Maxi, is that you?" The voice didn't sound familiar.

"Yes, this is Maxi. Who's this?" I try to compose myself quickly. People I did business with called on this line. The company's worth would drop if customers thought I was a lunatic.

"Maxi, this is Mary Swintek. Are you ok?"

"Yeah, I'm alright. How are you, Mary?" I switched to my touch business voice.

"I'm good, Max. The reason I'm calling is I haven't heard back from you regarding my fax. Did you get a chance to look at my recommendations?"

"Mary, refresh my memory, please. So much has been going on I haven't been to my office in a few days. Did you do another project?"

"Project, no. Nancy sent over some papers for me to review. You know, the ones regarding the sale of your business." I could hear the confusion in her voice. "So I took a look and faxed back a few questions and recommendations. Is that what you needed?"

Leave it to Nancy to try to cover my butt. As much as she hated Gert, I never thought she'd ignore my wishes. Chalk up another one to those who turn during adversity pile. It is me and only me against the world.

"Oh, those papers." I am going to kill Nancy when I saw her or better yet fire her. I could feel more tension slipping into my shoulders. "So, what do you think?" Knowing Nancy, she had already paid her so I might as well hear what she had to say.

"First off, I didn't realize you had a partner."

"Partner? No, this is a sole proprietorship."

"Interesting. According to the rider, all proceeds from the sale are to be electronically transferred to an off-shore account under the name Lenora G. O'Hara. Does that name sound familiar?"

"Lenora G. O'Hara, huh? What else does it say?" I asked. F-ing Gert. Nancy, Molly, and Jon had all been right about her.

"Well,, let's see. Proceeds are to be transferred to a bank in Cuba. Maxi, I wouldn't do that. It's going to be difficult to get your money back in the states when you need it."

"You're right. I shouldn't do that. Is there more?"

"Let's see what else stood out. Another clause says you are relinquishing all copyrights for future publications to Ms. O'Hara. Maxi, you should keep the copyrights to the publications in case the new owners cease operation. That way, you can start up again if you choose to. It will also get you a nice residual check if you decide to go that route. I'm surprised the buyer didn't insist on taking those. There is something else here that bugged me. Let me think," What else could there be? It sounded like Gert, aka Lenora G. O'Hara, took care of screwing me six ways to Sunday.

"Oh, here it is. I would remove this stipulation if anything happens to Ms. O'Hara; the proceeds revert over to a Hildegard O'Hara-Morgan."

"Who the hell is that?"

"Don't know. It's your agreement. Other than the amendment, everything else seems in order. Standard business sale with an employment contract attached. Not a very good one either. It says here you'll work as a rep on this project for a year. Does this sound, right?"

"No, it doesn't. The original agreement stated I was going to run this division."

"It is weird, Max. That was in the original I received, but for some reason, it was crossed out, and this new package inserted. I am not sure who did that."

"I think I know. By the way, is there an employment contract for Nancy Martin too?"

"No, there isn't, but the package contained a bunch of notes in your handwriting. Not sure if they were instructions or what, but none of it was executed in the agreement or the amendment."

I inhale to a count of ten, then slowly released the air. "Mary, could you do me a favor and draw up an amendment according to my notes? Also, I need the original package Fed-X'd as is, along with the new contract we discussed, by overnight mail. I'll give you a different address to send it to." I gave Nancy's home address. "Thank you for all your assistance. Oh, and you can send your bill to the same address." Nancy wrote the checks anyway if she hadn't already taken care of paying Mary.

"I'm glad I called. I will get right on this."

"I'm glad you called too." I hung up and dialed Nancy's cell. I didn't want to leave a message on her home machine, just in case.

"Darling, I'm so glad you called. Please leave me a message," her voice purred. I prayed I would have that woman's stamina when I am in my sixties.

"Nancy, first let me say you were right all along, and I was wrong. I will sign and date a piece of paper that says so, and you can hang it on the wall of your new office. And thank you for sending the paperwork to Mary Swintek. I was going to fire you when she called today, but instead, I'm going to give you a fat juicy raise! As usual, you saved my butt again. Now that I got the groveling out of the way, back to business. Mary is Fed-Xing a package to your house. Please don't ask me why. It has the revised paperwork we need for the sale. Do not give this to anyone but me. No one must know this except us." I hesitated then added, "I owe you. Call me on my cell."

Damn, I hate it when she is right. I'd never hear the end of this one. I hit myself upside the head again. I had forgotten to ask my mother about Pete. I didn't know whether I should call him next or Zack. Zack is closer, but Pete is my brother. I redialed Pete's cell and got a voice mail message again. "Pete, its Max. Listen, there are weird and scary things happening here, and this isn't about Zack calling or my love life. It's about real life. I really, really, need to speak to you. Please call me. Thanks."

I pressed end and looked out to the marina. The obnoxious cigarette boat from the other day had pulled in to the day dock. I watch as two men unload briefcases into a waiting white pickup truck. Why did

214

that truck look familiar? One of the men is super skinny with slicked-back hair. Was he on a boat? The other one could be a football lineman. He is much more casual in cut-offs and t-shirt. There is something familiar about them.

"Fucking Gert." She pissed me off. How could I have been so stupid? So, trusting? She was a stranger who showed up at my door. Maybe it hadn't been chutzpah, this was all part of some big plan from the beginning.

I watched the men load something else, some kind of package, and then a third one emerged from the cabin area. The other guy looks like Jon, my soon-to-be-ex. The latter I affectionately called a parasite on society's underwear, among other appropriate nicknames.

I viewed a little longer as the coolers, backpacks, and other containers were loaded into the bed of the truck. It must have been nice to be out on the river enjoying the relaxing summer heat as opposed to being kept inside a climate-controlled condo. I am totally suffocating. I want to open the windows, at least get the smell of the ocean. I wonder what would happen if I left. Would the guy in the van hold me hostage? Would it make Zack come back quicker?

I dialed Zack's cell and waited for him to answer. Just then, the back doorbell rang. It's probably a neighbor or Girl Scout selling cookies or Al finally showing up with the breakfast. I hit end before Zack picked up and bounce down the stairs. I am hoping for Girl Scout cookies. I felt safe answering since I had a bodyguard in a van watching me.

I open the door to find Gert standing there in shorts and a tank top holding her briefcase. Caught by surprise, I could only say, "Hey."

"Hey, yourself. Is this where you've been hiding out? I have been looking all over town for you. Have you shacked up with a new dude or what?"

She strutted right by me into the living room, plopped down on the sofa, and faced me. I had my back to the door.

Gert opened her briefcase on top of the coffee table. "We've got to file this paperwork. Mr. Carlson is not being a patient man," she stated with a laugh. "I don't know how you worked for that guy." I stood there a moment. I wanted to strangle her. My stomach did the summersault thing, and the little voice in my head whispered, "Tread lightly, Max." The calm demeanor, the slick clothes, the cat-like nails, everything about Gert suddenly made me want to regurgitate.

"You ok, Max? You look weird."

"Yeah, I'm fine." I sit in the chair opposite her. I could hear my cell phone ringing upstairs. I didn't want to go answer it because that would mean leaving Gert alone. For the first time since we met, I didn't want to turn my back on her.

"Ok, Well, I need your signature where the highlights are, then I can get these to Bob, and we will be done." She sat, smug and smiling. I looked down at the amendment, the amendment Mary had warned me about. That piece of paper gave Gert complete control of my company, total control of my money, full control of my life.

"Do we need to do this now? I can't think."

"Maxi, you don't need to think. You have me."

"Gert, I don't feel like doing this right now."

"Maxi, just sign the papers. It's not a big deal." Not a big deal to whom? What planet is she on? I got up and headed for the bathroom to buy some time to think.

"I'll be right back," I gestured toward the bathroom. "I was on my way in when you arrived." I shut the door behind me. One thing I definitely don't like about this condo is the first-floor bathroom lacked windows. I don't think I want to live here, after all.

"Maxi, is everything all right in there?" Gert sang from the living room. I used to love it when she got giddy over a deal. But at that moment, she made my stomach curdle.

"I'm fine. I'll be out in a minute." In the mirror, I freaked out. I didn't know what to do next. So, I made faces in the mirror: wide eyes, open mouth, fake scream look, and a big smile. Gert couldn't be that bad. She'd been my best friend and confidant for years. This couldn't be happening. People didn't just screw you over after years of friendship, did they?

"Deep breaths, Max. Just say no." I put on my best fierce girl look, pry open the door, with shoulders back I walk into the living room.

"The papers, Max." Gert slid the pile towards me. I never noticed Gert had such vacant eyes. I had to admit, her fierce girl look is a lot better than mine. And she still sat there with a painted-on grin.

"How was your weekend?" There is nothing like the old change-the-subject routine. It had always worked for me with my mom and my business associates.

"Sign the papers, Max." My hand started to shake visibly. I tried to peek out the window. Gert watched everything I did like she was trying to read my mind. She once told me the reason she was so good at being a lawyer is because of her psychic powers. I wondered how true this might be.

"Actually, I decided not to sell. I thought it over and decided I needed to keep my business, so there will be something normal after the divorce is over. I think this is pretty smart of me, huh?" I faked a smile.

Gert moved closer to me. "Max, I'm asking you for the last time to sign the papers." She glanced over my shoulder, so I turned around and surprise! There is Luke, my soon to be ex's attorney, standing in the doorway pointing a gun at me. Great!

I turn back to Gert. "What the….?"

"Come on, Max. You are a smart woman." Hillsey's laugh came from behind. "I know you figured it out. You even went out and hired another attorney. I saw the fax when we went through your office. You're a lot better at hiding things than I thought. And a lot smarter than I gave you credit for. Come on, sign the papers, and no one gets hurt."

Pond scum and Gert had the advantage. I looked back at Luke. "Why?"

"It's just business," She shrugged. I took the papers in my trembling hands, but I couldn't do it.

"Gert," I pleaded.

"Lenora, can't I shoot her and shut her up. I mean, you did have her sign the new will, right?" Luke's tapped his foot impatiently like I am keeping him from a meeting or a dinner date or maybe a shower.

218

Gert looked back at me and got a creepy smile on her face. "Yeah, she signed it, but this way is more legit, plus I don't have to deal with that sniveling kid. And please do not call me that, darling, not now at least."

Darling? I am going to be sick. And she thought she would get custody of Ric? What the heck is happening?

"Gert…"

"Maxi…"

Another muffled voice came in from outside the door. I could see Jon's face peeking in, and all at once, my frustrations began to pour out. "You lying piece of shit. How could you do this to me? I took care of you. I gave you everything! I was going to give you half, but no. You You You…"

"Get rid of him! Get him out of here!" Gert yelled to someone outside. I heard a gun go off and then another man walked in. Oh my, hey, there is my delivery person, damn, what's his name. Nancy is right again. I would have to trust her gut more in the future if I lived to see her in the future.

"All set," he announced with a smile. "He's gone, and nothing's going to bring him back." He giggled. "Finally got rid of that whiny pain in the…. Can we go now? If she doesn't sign, stick her on the boat. We can dump her in the sound, too."

"Good idea." Gert turned to face me again. "Maxi, you should know it wasn't supposed to be this way. When I set up the sale, I was to be the only contact, but then Bob Carlson wanted to work through you. Loyalty. Go figure." She leaned in close than in a stage whisper added, "You were just to be taken for a ride. But now..."

Did she set up the sale? Bob Carlson hadn't noticed my guides prior? This is worse than I thought. Now Gert crushed my ego too. "I am a total loser. I mean, really. I can't keep a husband. Apparently, I have a lousy business, employees leave me, so-called friends stab me in the back. I'm a gossip topic in the town I live in. Hell, the only thing I do have is my kid. I think I'm a good mom. Maybe I'm not..."

"Can't you shut her up?" Luke yelled, blocking his ears with both hands. "We need to get out of here."

I wonder where my bodyguard went to, the one in the van who is supposed to be watching me. Something must have happened because Zack said if I left, I wouldn't make it past the front sidewalk. I couldn't believe the goon wouldn't notice a gun going off or all these people hanging around outside my door. Oh crap.

My brain went on complete overload, and my face reddened. The only thing I could think to do is to reach out and kick Gert in the shin as hard as I could. She screamed, then toppled over, holding her knee. I ran to the front door and attempted to wedge it open. The door is stuck, probably from the damn summer humidity.

I turn in time to see the big guy carry Gert out the back door. The front door won't move. I can't get the sucker open. I pulled with all my might. I banged to get my bodyguard's attention. Some bodyguard he is. He had decided to take a nap in the front seat.

"Hey, Maxi!" I turn in time to see the Tart in my doorway. She lifted the gun in her hand and squeezed

220

the trigger. My shoulder went on fire. My shirt turned the same dark shade of crimson that my face was earlier. "Waste of air," I heard her say right before the dots appeared. They were not even the pretty dots. These were all gray, and some were black.

Chapter Twenty-Four

"Jerry, play that guitar!" I shout—my voice echoes. My arm hurt. I must have whacked it somewhere. Oh, Well,. "La la la la WHEEEEEEEEEEEE!" having so much fun. I loved the bright lights and the loud music, and "Who are you?" Right above me stood a purple lady. She smiled down at me. Her hands were moving all around. It looked like she is adjusting my body, how weird is that? Do you think she could make my arm stop hurting? I mean, that could be nice. Why worry? I believe it is best to go back to music and blue stars.

I wondered what time Zack would get here. Just like in high school, my thoughts turned to him. He pops into my brain. Why? Why? Why must I do this? "Why?" I heard myself giggle. What a weird voice I had.

Back to high school. All the possibilities, all the anguish, all the unimportant crap that seemed like life and death way back then. Would Zack ask me to the prom? Would Zack talk to me in science class? Or better yet, why didn't Zack speak to me today? I giggled again.

Would Zack and I lasted past graduation if we had gotten together in eighth grade? Or if we got together our senior year? What about after college?

Probably not. I wasn't as anal then. Had I become regimented or as my brother liked to say anal about things? Did I convert for Zack? I ended up doing something like partying because I wanted to be around him, so changing anything about me was in my realm of reality. Then again, I thought Zack was always a pretty regimented person. I could remember his parents making him take a class to get higher SAT scores in our junior year. Back in the 80s, that wasn't heard of. These days it's the norm or at least, so I am told by the other parents who sit in the stands at my son's sports events. I find out I do a lot of wrong things as a parent at those places.

I pray for the divorce … Wait, am I getting divorced from Zack? That would be pretty stupid on my part. Have you seen that dude's body? Wait a minute. Wouldn't my hand hit my head? Oh, look, I am wired. Wired? Cool. I bet the purple lady did it. I looked again. My mom and dad were in chairs a few feet away. They are talking, but I can't hear them. Ha. Ha. Ha. This is good. So, where am I? Oh yeah, the divorce and everything else that is happening could be screwing up my kid. Of course, how could he not be messed up? I had been worried since the day Ric was born, I was going to break him.

Please God, don't let all this crapola his dad put us though be a lifetime of baggage for him. He's so young. He's so vulnerable. He doesn't deserve any of this. God, I have a great kid. Love his smile. Let's see if I can do the smile. Ready. Stretch the lips across my face. Can't get the eyes opened wide, oh Well,, that's life.

A rush of heat hit my arm along with a trail of blue dots. I wondered where that came from. There is another arm next to mine. Blue dots. That must be Zack's arm. Where did he come from? The sea blue cotton sheet fell to the side. The moonlight from the window illuminated our bodies. His skin touched mine. The only sound I hear is soft, steady breathing coming from Zack and somewhere in the distance a quiet, beep, beep, beep.

Zack is so good. He probably felt good back in high school, too though I don't think at the time I would know the difference. His rhythmic breath comforted me. I watched his silhouette on the wall move up and down. I placed my hand on his stomach. I wanted to soak in the sensation. Zack is so hard, reliable, and dependable. The bad boy exterior melted away with a gentle touch. I had been waiting all my life for someone like him. I just didn't know it.

Beep.

Beep.

Beep.

His leg hairs brush against mine as he rolls over, pinning parts of my body under his. His leg wraps around mine. His arm slung around my waist. His nose snuggled up in my neck, and I got hot spots from soft kisses. Every place he moved, he left a spot of warmth. I turned my face towards his. His eyes appeared half-open. I breathed his breath in. I loved it when he smiled, and he got crinkles around his eyes and mouth. I'd like to think he only smiled that way for me.

"Hi," he whispers. He shifts his leg, sliding it down between mine.

"Hi," I try to bring my hips closer. I don't want space.

The angle of his face has his five o'clock stubble rubbing my chin, conflicting with the softness of his lips. I could taste salt and Zack and something else. He tasted good. I remembered our first kiss from that night at the restaurant. He just showed up at my parents' house unannounced. It seemed like months ago, yet only like a week had passed since he sauntered back into my life. And I allowed him back in.

The annoying beeps were getting faster and louder. The beep in the background had quietly entered the back of my mind. My body moved to press closer to his. I didn't want any space between us. I needed to be connected. I had been waiting so long, probably since we first met, to feel this man next to me, to feel his hardness against my softness, for him to be inside me.

Beep, beep, beep, beep….

Gosh, he is slowly draining my mind. I am turning into a blank canvas, and Zack is the master painter. His touch sent jolts of electricity through my body with each stroke of his brush. I could feel his hands move across my back, my shoulders, my stomach, my breasts.

I had waited for a lifetime. God, he feels so good. My horoscope told me he would come. I should believe more.

"Maxi," he whispered. "Maxi, are you there?"

"Yes," I answered. "I'm here, Zack." I could hear the beep clear and loud. BEEP. BEEP. BEEP. BEEP.

"Maxi, answer me."

What was he talking about? Is he deaf? I purred, "Yes, Zack, I am here."

"Come on, Max, wake up! Are you there?" Someone is shaking my arm! The one that hurt. It is pissing me off! The voice grew louder. I could no longer feel Zack's touch! The noise is disturbing. BEEP! BEEP! BEEP! BEEP!

"Come on, Maxi! Open those beautiful eyes!" My lids lay heavy — so much work to open them. The room is all fuzzy, and my eyes refused to focus.

Okay, now where is Zack? Where did he go? "Zack?" My voice is hoarse like a cigarette smoker's or like a voice that hadn't been used for a long time. Someone held my left hand, but I couldn't feel my right. At least it didn't hurt anymore.

"Right here, Maxi. I'm right here." Zack's voice called. He is getting clearer now. I felt strokes of heat over my hand. I looked in the direction of blue speckles and saw a hand touching mine. The flecks were Zack's fingers! I forced my eyes up to his arm, up to his face. He had on his worried look, the one where the horizontal lines across his nose stuck out. I'd seen that look a lot since we started hanging out again. Like when those wackadoodles broke into my house or into my office.

His face is changing. He watched me, then his lips went from straight across to turn up. Yeah. It's the crinkled eyes smile. I loved the crinkled eyes smile! "I am so happy to see you!" he said softly.

Zack brought his lips down to kiss me on the cheek. There is a row of machines and lights behind him. Red and green lights move up and down like on my stereo receiver. Wow, those lights are cool. Although I didn't think they were playing music. One of the machines made the beeps. The beeps had slowed again, quietly, in the distance. Beep...Beep…Beep.

226

My head is massive and turning it in the other direction, hard—pain shot through my arm. An unfamiliar voice instructed, "Don't move, Mary Alexis. Please. You'll pull your stitches out." I couldn't see who is speaking or who would call me Mary Alexis except for my mother when she's pissed about something, or the nuns in Sunday school. I didn't see any habits around. Of course, I could have done something to piss my mother off. I couldn't think of what, but the possibility always existed.

"Mary Alexis, I said stop…" Oh my gosh, it is my friend, the purple lady.

"Hi." I sounded wasted. "Yay, the purple lady is back." I sang out loud. My mom and dad were in the room, too, standing next to Zack. Man, did they look old. When did they get gray hair? Bet I'd get blamed for those. Not my brothers, though. Pete and Matt are perfect. I am a perfect screw up. "Yep, that's me," I giggled. My mother appeared like she had been crying. Her eyes were red and swollen. At least she is not pissed at me unless she is so mad she had burst into tears. If that is the case, I needed to get out of here fast because I am in big trouble. Crap. What had I done this time?

Beep……Beep…….Beep.

"Maxi, honey, you were hurt. You are going to be ok." Zack spoke softly. His balmy breath felt so good. I wish they all would leave so we could go back to bed. I wanted to suck his smell. That was so nice to be in bed next to him. I am making myself really hot. I try to kick off my covers. They won't budge. Am I tied down?

I used my energy to open my eyes wide. The room is unfamiliar, and it smelled like cleaning fluid. "Where the hell am I?" I heard myself ask. The lady dressed in purple scrubs reached above me. Something cold is moving up into the arm as Zack rubbed.

"You're at Middlesex," Mom said as if I should know. She leans over my bed. I follow her arm to see she is holding my other hand. I can't feel her touch! White gauze is wrapped around my upper arm. Blood soaked through in spots. Oh gosh. My stomach flip-flopped. I think I might puke.

"Middlesex? No, I am at a condo." My head hurt. "Where's Ric?"

"Ric is fine. He's with your brother Matt and hanging out with his cousins." My mom managed a heavy smile. "I'm going to call and let him know you're awake. I can bring him by to see you tomorrow." My mother disappeared.

Dad leaned over to kiss me on the forehead. This must be big because my dad doesn't do hospitals, not even when my mother goes in. "I'll call Pete and let him know you're okay too."

"Freakin', Pete." I turn my head back to Zack. "Wasn't I at a condo? Gert, you, and me drinking green champagne from the water fountain." My eyes squinted. "We were at a condo, weren't we?" The cleaning fluid smell grew more potent, and my stomach churned. If I cleaned the house more often, I'd be used to it. Then again, maybe not. Some people weren't put on earth to clean.

"Yep, you were." Zack sighed. "Max, do you remember anything?"

Yeah, I remember your kisses and your touch and your body melting with mine. And running, or was that a figment of my imagination?

"No," I said, then I saw a shadow move past the doorway; it entered into my room carrying flowers. Lots of flowers. "Pretty," I managed to get out. "Were you at the condo?"

"Not when this happened." Zack brushed his lips against my cheek. The blue sparkles were back. My cheeks tightened as my pain killer dazed smile took over my face. "Maxi, I am so sorry. There was never violence in other cases. I thought it would be alright but...I...I'm so sorry. Maxi, get some rest." As those lips pressed against my forehead, I fell back asleep and headed back towards the concert.

Chapter Twenty-Five

I was a total waste case for three days. On my first coherent day, I was both excited and scared. The purple nurse, whose name I learned was Laura, took out my drug tube, so all I had to stop my pain were tiny yellow pills. I like the machine with the magic button a lot better. I had only been without it for one morning. It wasn't going to work. Laura had snuck in before I woke up to steal my magic. Perhaps she knew I wouldn't relinquish it without a fight.

My room is too bright with its obnoxious florescent lights and a window facing south. The set-up is perfect for the bright disgusting morning sun. I keep asking to leave. "I need to watch you a few more days to be sure you're stable," the stupid doctor said. Like I am ever stable! Zack covered my mouth with his hand before I could respond. Good move on his part since a four-letter unladylike word is sitting on the tip on my tongue.

It is good the room is bright because, with dim lighting, the place would look like a funeral parlor. There were flowers everywhere. Nancy had sent beautiful purple daisies. Bob Carlson sent a Get Well, bouquet from FTD. I could guarantee that Joanne, his assistant ordered it. I made a mental note to send her a thank you too. My wonderful son Ric brought in a big huge vase filled with wildflowers he had picked from our neighbor's yard. There were red roses with a teddy bear from my parents, and a card from Pete and his family. His wife spent the minimum on us. If I had been a blood relative to her, I'd be overwhelmed with stuff. She might even visit. I guess being blood to my brother had its positive points.

There are a teddy bear and candy from Matt, my other brother, and his family. Right by my bed sat two dozen purple roses from Zack. Not to mention cards hanging all around. My nephew in college even sent one. That should have told me this is a big deal. I guess it's not every day I get shot.

It's nice to be loved.

I knew I am near the end of my stay because the nurse came in once in the morning and wouldn't be back until after lunch. My phone stopped ringing, and from what I gathered, my family and friends had gone back to their lives. I sit by myself, surrounded by stuff when I need people. It reminded me of when Ric was born. On my last day in the hospital, I had no visitors. By the time Jon finally came to pick me up at five in the evening, I was in tears, and he couldn't figure out why.

Jon never got it. It is sad the way it all ended for him. From what I was told, he was killed after I was shot. Knowing Jon, he probably shot off his mouth and got shot in the process. I wonder if Hillsey did him in. It would be perfect if the Tart did in the slime.

I still find it hard to believe Gert and Hillsey are sisters. What kind of gene pool is that? And Hillsey was allowed to reproduce! God help us when those two grow up. Imagine what they've learned from their mother and aunt. They could write a book called *How*

To Scam People In Five Easy Steps. I'd never admitted this, but I should have listened to Molly and Nancy and even Jon. They all knew. How they knew, I'd never understand. Gert seemed so lovely. She was kind to me. She worked hard. She became my best friend. She turned out to be a con artist. You know, I am way too nice.

I will always wonder when Jon found out the nasty details and how long he let it all go on. That question would never be answered. I heard when people die, there is always one question left that loved ones to want to ask. In my case, although there was no love left, I still wanted to know why. What did I ever do to deserve the crap he pulled on me? Or better yet, besides being born, what did Ric do? Jon was an idiot.

Technically I am still his wife, so I guess I will need to organize a funeral. My mom told me not to worry about it. She agreed it would be bad karma not to do something. Everyone, no matter how much of a slime they are, deserved to be sent on to the next life with some dignity. I wish I wasn't the one who had to do it.

"Hey, are we having a pity party here?" I looked up to see Zack standing in my doorway. God, he is gorgeous. Then I get a glimpse of someone standing behind him.

"I'm trying, but you just spoiled all the fun!" And made my day in the process. "Are you here to take me away from all this? I can be dressed and ready to go in record time. I just need a lift."

"Nope. Doc said you are here for one more night." I hold up my middle finger. "Cute, Max. Hey, I did bring a surprise…" Zack stepped aside and in strolled my brother Pete in his full Navy dress uniform.

"Freakin', Pete." I smile. After all my voicemails, pages, and text messages, my brother had finally gotten back to me, in person no less.

"I'm not really here." That is code for *don't tell anyone I'm in town.* "When I got Zack's message, I took a transport back. I wanted to see you as soon as I could."

"Transport from where? Do you know how many times I called?" I crossed my arms over my chest for emphasis. I am provoking an argument I had no chance of winning. It didn't matter where Pete was. It only mattered than he was worried enough to be here to visit me. I could live with that.

"Actually, I do, Max, and I'm sorry. I knew you were in good hands…" Pete glanced over at Zack, who had sat down in one of the visitors' chairs. "I'm here now. That's got to count for something." Pete moved closer to give me a gentle hug. He stunk like he hadn't showered in days. I got teary-eyed.

"It does." I had so many questions, but half I couldn't ask with Zack sitting there. "Did ya hear? We have matching bullet holes!" Pete had been shot during one of his missions about ten years back. He still hadn't told me what he was doing, and I no longer wanted to know.

"Yeah, I heard. You tried to play the hero…"

"No, I decided Gert needed a swift kick. I never thought a friend would shoot me. I thought it was the client's job to shoot the lawyer."

Pete nudged me over to fit on the mattress next to me. "So what does she know?" he directed the question to Zack.

"Well,, let's see....She knows Gert and Hillsey are sisters and scam artists who tried to bankrupt her."

"I know I don't need to get divorced anymore because Jon was shot by one of them," I add, trying not to smirk. Pete nodded and looked back at Zack.

"The same people were behind all the robberies. Besides the two women, there was Ms. Fontaine's husband…"

"Zack, Gert was a widow," I corrected.

"Remember the guys' Nancy didn't want to hire to do deliveries?" I nodded. "He was Ms. Fontaine's current, not dead husband, along with her sister's current husband." My mouth fell open wide. "Did either of them look familiar? Ms. Fontaine's husband was also Jon's divorce lawyer, and he was the one who had the license to practice in Connecticut. She didn't have a law degree, never mind license to practice." I got a sick feeling in my stomach as I recalled how Luke and Gert would gawk at each other during meetings. "You are lucky you had Nancy. If she hadn't sent the sale paperwork for your business deal to Newport, we might have never been tipped off. When Gert finally came after you at the condo, it was because she found out you were advised differently on the sale. She would have lost at least a million dollars, if not more."

"How did she find out?"

"They broke into your house again, and there was a fax sitting on the machine in your home office. I think that's when they decided to move everything up." Zack stretched while in motion towards the door. "I'll leave you two alone for a few."

"Wait, don't go."

234

"It's okay," said Pete. "I'm only here for about an hour; then, Zack needs to get me back to Bradley. I was worried about you."

"I was worried about you too."

"So why all the pages?" Pete's sense of humor is slightly more warped than mine. "What was the emergency? By the way, the guys thought the message about me being self-centered while you went off about your life was hysterical."

"Thanks. Glad to provide entertainment for our troops." I'd punch him in the arm if I had the strength. "Anything I need to worry about?" I decide to keep the conversation light. I could ask him about Zack another time.

Pete rubbed his eyes. He has dark circles underneath. This is probably his only day off, and here he is with me. "Not anymore. Zack and I met up in DC last year sometime, and he mentioned he was working on a big embezzlement case. Although I had a few details of what the case entailed, it sounded familiar."

"So, you sent Zack to me?" Damn, I knew this was just business.

"Like this is a hardship for either of you," Pete laughed. Ok, he got me there. "I told Zack you were getting a divorce, nothing more. I guessed when they profiled Ms. Fontaine, your name came up. He got lucky."

"No, he didn't," I countered. But he might if he played his cards right.

"That is not what I meant. I mean, he got lucky looking you up." I am about to comment when Pete continued, "Zack owes you this case, Max."

I silently contemplated this new revelation. Zack owed me. Not quite what I wanted.

"Why are you shaking your head, no?" Pete scrutinized me.

"I'm not sure I want Zack to owe me."

"What do you want, Max?" Zack is leaning in the doorway, illuminated by the lighting.

"Yeah, Max, what do you want?" Pete echoed. I could tell it is time for him to go because he stood up to wait for my answer.

"I want…" I paused to buy thinking time. God, this was hard. Sometimes *I'm in love with you* were the hardest words in the English language to say. "I want things to be normal."

Zack gave Pete a look then turned towards me, "Normal before or normal now?"

"Normal now."

"Good." Zack moved quickly to kiss me on the lips. Wow-eee. He reluctantly pulled away so Pete could lean over and give me a kiss on the cheek goodbye.

"Take care of her," Pete ordered.

Zack saluted my brother and added, "Yes, sir. Max, I'll be back."

"And remember, I wasn't here," Pete repeated. If I were still on the good pain killers, I might chalk this all up as a dream. But I am glad I am only taking the little yellow pills.

Acknowledgments

- I am lucky to be partnered with one of the best upcoming editors, Amanda Pampuro. Thank you for putting up with my creative endeavors.
- I would also like to thank the CoLoNY chapter of Romance Writers of America. This group of dynamic individuals has been encouraging and inspiring throughout my writing process.
- Thank you to the academics and motivators, which wouldn't let me quit: Christine Archer, Kay Janney, & Jamie Callan.
- To my happy hour partners – thank you for diversions, doses of reality, and telling me I am not crazy.
- Most importantly, thank you to my family – because, without their love and support, this wouldn't be happening!

There are others – too many to name, who have shown love support, & encouragement. Thank you with all my heart!

Their story continues…

Maximum Trouble, available now!

Moist droplets of fluid compressed along Zack Brady's hairline as the reverberation of his work boots clamor against the metal stairs within the tight, dank space. He moved with purpose towards the lit exit sign. With force, he pushed the door. Bright sunlight reflected up across the colossal pavement. The heat hit his body with full force. Zack put on his aviators and waited a minute for his eyes to focus. To his right, a massive military jet saddled up to the hanger he exited. On his left, a field bordered by electric fencing. Totally exposed, his destination lay in front—the two-story brick building with a metal connector to another hanger. No planes visibly attached. All doors and windows shut tight.

He sucked in a deep breath. On the exhale, all his attention focused on the path he considered necessary to take. With shoulders back and head held high, he started to walk in the direction of his objective.

"Excuse me, sir," Zack swore under his breath, "May I see your—" He turned in the direction of the young Military Police Officer. The MP's eyes move up and down his dated uniform. Zack waited. The M.P. raised his hand to a salute, "I'm sorry, sir, please continue."

Zack dismissed him with a quick salute. Without a word, he resumed his trek. He turned back to catch the young soldier speaking into his radio. From memory, his strides lengthened as his pace quickened.

He hesitated a breath before opening the windowless metal door. Cold air refreshed his wet face. Bumps developed on his neck with a chill replacing the heat within his body. He allowed his thoughts to drift to Maxi and her family. Once again, he needed to get her out of a jam.

He did a quick scan of the room as Maxi's smile entered his brain. The dentist's office furniture arranged around the perimeter broke only to reveal a door with a phone. He crossed the room in two strides to pick up the receiver. A woman's voice garbled through the handset.

"State your business," she barked.

"I need to see the Admiral now."

His request returned with silence.

Zack waited as the shadows moved behind a large mirror on the wall adjacent to the door. His heartbeat increased. He turned back to the door outside. He silently counted the seconds. One glance went to his wrist armor, C28, to note the actual time.

Knowledge gave him three minutes. His experience brought the number to two.

Another shadow joined the group. He had been on the opposite side of the mirror many times. On the other side, this group held a debate about what to do next. His situation could only go in two directions; he either meets with the admiral or is under arrest. He couldn't see the man, yet he knew the M.P. he met crossing the tarmac stood on the opposing side of his escape.

Both scenarios possessed the same level of pressure. He had been thrown in the brig before and hadn't much liked it. Zack needed to move. He paced out ten strides from corner to corner within the confine of the room. He started on a diagonal, changed to walk the parameter, all the while exercising the same step count. Zack inhaled and exhaled to the rhythm of his steps. His arms tucked against his body, although at each corner, he wiggled the fingers on each hand. He observed more shadows in the mirror. Now an outline he recognized. Broad shoulders, thick torso, with a slim pointed device coming off the right side. "Crap," he muttered aloud.

His body involuntarily let out a jump at the door buzzer. He entered to expectations. Military Police flanked both sides of an older, attractive female. She stood with a Well, practiced look of neutrality on her face. Zack folded his hands in plain view. He stood military at ease to wait for her to speak first, not wanting to give anything away.

A military police officer moved behind him to block the exit. The other stayed at attention next to the female, hand resting on his sidearm.

"We've been waiting for you, Mr. Brady," the woman said, without further explanation, adding, "Boys, please escort our friend to the Admiral's conference room." The two men moved to either side of Zack. "Oh, and make certain he is relieved of his weapon before entering the secured area." Zack felt a hand slipped down his back as the pressure from his firearm disappeared. They patted him down the sides to remove another gun and the knife from his boot. One of the M.P.'s commented, "Nice," as the other displayed the weapon. The mystery woman left through an inconspicuous door on the left.

"This way please," one M.P. pointed towards the more prominent door. In the mirrored reflection, the officer stood behind him, his weapon by his side. He acknowledged the directive with a nod to proceed.

"Today must be your lucky day," one of the M.P.'s said.

"I hope so," Zack replied. "I sure hope so."

Available at Pampuro.com and your local, independent bookseller.

Also, by L.M. Pampuro,
Dancing with Faith
Maximum Mayhem (Zack & Maxi's 1st adventure)
The Perfect Pitch
Passenger: the only game in town
Uncle Neddy's Funeral
Maximum Trouble
Harlot's grace
Harlot's fire
Visit her at Pampuro.com